TALES OF TH

TALES OF THE SEAL PEOPLE

Scottish Folk Tales

DUNCAN WILLIAMSON

Illustrated by Chad McCail

INTERLINK

First American edition published in 1992 by
INTERLINK BOOKS
An imprint of Interlink Publishing Group, Inc.
99 Seventh Avenue
Brooklyn, New York 11215

Published simultaneously by Canongate Press plc, Edinburgh

Library of Congress Cataloging-in-Publication Data available

ISBN 1–56656–101–9 (hbk)
ISBN 0–940793–99–7 (pbk)

Printed and bound in Great Britain

To my dear friends Stephanie and Sheila

Contents

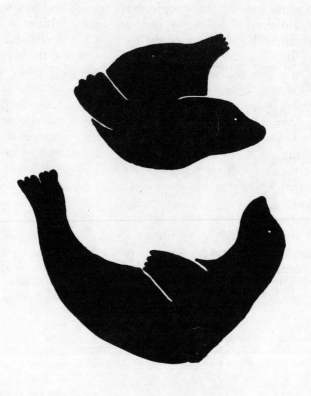

Introduction

IN ALL MY COLLECTIONS of stories from Scotland, the
most beautiful are those that have been told to me by the
fishermen and crofting folk of the West Coast. And these stories
are of the seal people. Now many listeners have asked me questions, where are the seal people, who are the seal people and
where did they begin? I say they are *silkies*. This is a word
derived from 'silky', meaning the softness of the seal skin. My
granny had a piece of seal-skin. It can forecast the weather:
before a storm the hair rises up telling you it's going to be
rough; when the sun comes out the seal-skin lies smooth and
soft and silky. Not all seals are silkies, but some have the power
to take over the form of a human being, be a human, or take
away a human to become a seal. To have the command of being
one of the seal people, your mother or father must have married
one of the seal-folk. A human makes love to the seal — not as
an animal — but as a person, a seal-woman or a seal-man.
Children who are born of a human and a seal have the power
to transform into either, be a human or be a seal.

But the importance of the silkie is its part in the Other World,
or after-life. For instance, if you were a fisherman and you lived
with your daddy in a little croft by the seaside, and you had
your brother, your grandfather or your uncle lost at sea; what
would you do if their body was not found? Isn't it a terrible
thought that maybe he was lying there at sea, never got a decent
burial, the words of God never said over him — he was never
to be found. But if you thought for one instant that your
brother, your uncle or your grandfather never returned because
he had joined the seal people, he'd become one of them; then
how would you feel? There are many beautiful seal stories about
people returning after ten years lost at sea but not one single
day older. We believed they had joined the seal people.

Now this is the legend. That's why it was told. To make
people feel comforted if their loved ones were never found.
They probably joined the seal people, became seal folk. And
you'll see them again. I was doing a session in the Hopeman

1

Library up on the Moray Firth and I explained to the children what seal stories were about. This child of twelve, a bonnie little boy with hazel eyes and curly hair came up to me after the session was finished. He said, 'Mr Williamson, you made me very happy.' I said, 'Why, son, did you like the stories?' He said, 'Mr Williamson, I loved your stories. They were beautiful. But you see I lost my daddy in the Hopeman tragedy. Mr Williamson, maybe my daddy's joined the seal people and I'll see him again.' There was a trawler lost at sea in late 1985. Seven men were lost; five were found, but two were never.

When I was a child I was reared by the sea. I ate everything that hopped, jumped or crawled in the sea. I loved the seals. And I spent a night on an island with them. They came in lying around me grunting and greeting, and one old fellow was crying with toothache all night, although I did not know it at the time. It was only years later when I spent some time with an old fisherman, and he told me why the old fellow was crying! My father was also very fond of the seals. He used to play the bagpipes to them. He would play a tune to the seals, and they would all pop their heads out of the water, stand up straight listening. It was the greatest thing in the world to see fifteen, twenty seals gathered listening, all looking every different direction! Because seals are awful fond of music, any kind, even whistling or singing. That's what attracted travelling folk to the seals in the first place. The travelling people really believed in the seals. My father believed they would come at night and throw stones at you, at the camps, if you were bad to them during the day. The seals or silkies will never do you any harm, not unless you are bad to them. Then they set out to teach you a lesson. If you are good to them then all good things happen, you get what you want. Silkies are only out to protect their own families, the same as the travellers.

In the past, privileged camping for the travelling people was on the shore-sides. A large part of many travellers' lives was spent camped right on the beaches. All that was seen to people passing by on the road was smoke coming from their fires. But the local folk knew the camping places, and it was natural at night for a lonely old fisherman or crofter coming along the shoreside from a bar-room, who saw the tinkers' fire, to come into the campsite with a bottle of whisky in his pocket. He sat down by the travellers' fireside and gave the old men a drink, and he probably told a story! This is how some seal stories were passed down to my people.

But I learned most of the seal stories I know directly from working with crofters and fishermen along Loch Fyne. These people didn't frankly tell stories to just anybody. They had very guarded attitudes towards their knowledge. It was sacred information, told to them by their family and they meant to keep it in their family. It was only by me partly coaxing them and by accident and my being interested that I ever opened them up to get one seal story from them! Now the important thing to remember is that these stories were never *made*, they were never set to any pattern. They were just 'something strange' according to them that actually took place. It was family history, that's the truth.

I have felt privileged all my life to have heard these stories from the people of my homeland. At the time I never gave it a thought that I would tell it again to audiences, or one day be a 'storyteller'. But even at the age of thirteen I knew that these crofters and fishermen in their sixties, and older, were giving me something private and something special. Stories from tradition are magic — because they are given to you as a present — you are let into the personal lives of your friends. You are accepted as one of the family. It is my deepest responsibility to tell the story again to you with the love and respect for their forbears.

THE SILKIE PAINTER

Sealfolk are supposed to help you, do good things for you.
They've never been known to do anyone any evil! So the story
I'm going to tell you is about an old woman and a seal. It
was told to me many many years ago by a man who believed
that this really happened. His name was Neil MacCallum, the
old stonemason I was apprenticed to when I was fifteen at
Auchindrain. It was a story kept in his family and ours. The
Highlanders were a very close-knitted kind of folk and didn't
go telling the whole world about their stories and tales and
cracks because people would have thought they were crazy.
But Neil maintained that his great-great-granny told him this
one because she had the picture in her house . . .

MANY YEARS AGO on the West Coast there lived an old fisherman and his wife. They had this wee cottage by the shore-side. The fisherman used to set his nets, and what fish he and the old woman couldn't use he took along to the village and sold. The old woman kept a couple of goats and some hens; she used to sell eggs and goat's milk in the village. In the small village where they stayed there was only one post office, a hotel and a small police station, and everybody knew everybody else. But they never had any family — the old folk lived pretty well by themselves. The old man only had one enemy, the seals. He hated the seals because they used to tear his nets and eat the fish. He couldn't stand seals in any way.

And he was always getting on to the old woman and telling her, 'That's another seal,' he would say, 'Mary. That's another good fish destroyed by these seals again, these animals! They're making a terrible mess of my nets. I wish to God they would clear out and never come back. I hate these terrible beasties!'

But the old woman, she was a kindly old cratur. She said, 'Well, John, you know they have to live just the same as every-body else.'

In her spare time the old woman used to gather seaweed, the dulse that comes in with the tide — these big thick stems of seaweed that break away with the heavy storms, with the work-ing of the sea. And the old woman used to collect these big thick tangles and stack them up to dry. When they were dry a man used to come and buy them from her. He sent them away to the towns to get made into perfume or whatever.

One day the old woman was down on the beach. She was as usual gathering seaweed and putting it out on the beach to dry, when she came over behind this rock. The first thing she saw was a wee baby seal, a newborn, two or three days she thought it to be. So she bent over to pick it up and said, 'Poor little thing.' She looked all around her to see if its mother or any other seals were about before picking it up, but she never saw another seal. So she thought to herself, I think maybe I'd better leave it. She just left it and walked away a wee bit . . . then she took another thought. And she walked back, picked it up. She had one of those rubber aprons for keeping her legs dry for picking up the seaweed, so she lifted up the apron and put the baby seal in it, held it in front of her and walked home.

By the time she walked home to the wee cottage at the shoreside, her old man had pulled up the boat. He was back and in a rage again. He was in a very bad mood because the seals had been at his nets, made holes in them and ate most of his good fish.

When the old woman came walking up, 'Well,' he said, 'Mary, you're back again.'

'Aye, John, I'm back.' She said, 'You look terrible. What's wrong?'

'Och,' he said, 'it's these seals! I'll have to get a gun and shoot them.'

'You know, John,' she said, 'I don't like you shooting seals.'

'Well,' he said, 'what else can I do? They're making a terrible mess of my nets: we'll have to do something about them.'

'Well,' she said, 'come on in anyway and we'll have a cup of tea.'

So they walked in. She had her apron rolled up in front of her.

He looks. 'Mary, what's that you've got there?'

She says, 'John, it's a baby seal.'

He said, 'What! Have you got a baby seal? You mean to tell me you've brought back a baby seal, here to this house, to me, when you know I don't like these animals!'

She says, 'John, it's lost its mother.'

'Well,' he said, 'woman, you keep it away from me or it'll lose more than its mother. Because you know I hate these things. What are you going to do with it anyway?'

'Well,' she said, 'John, I thought, seeing it lost its mother, that I would try to rear it up for a wee bit till it gets strong enough and then put it back in the sea.'

'Of course,' he said, 'but you'd be better to take a walking-stick and hit it at the back of the neck! If you make it strong enough and big enough it'll just go back to the sea and be one more to eat the fish in my nets.'

'Oh, well,' old Mary said, she was a kindly soul, 'well, if that happens, it happens. But I'm not going to do anything to the baby seal.'

Away she went and got an old creel and she put some straw in it. She put the baby seal down by the fire and went round by the back of the shed where she milked a goat. She had a teat and bottle for feeding young goats; she filled it full of goat's milk and fed it to the baby seal. The baby seal sucked the bottle of milk and lay contented by the fire.

So the old man, he's sitting and he's watching the seal; and old Mary's sitting at the other side of the fire. 'Now, woman, you know that I don't like these animals,' he said, 'and I just can't have you having it here!'

'Well, John, what am I going to do with it?' she said. 'You know fine I want to keep it warm.'

'Ach,' he said, 'keep it warm — put it out in the shed beside the goats.'

'No,' she said, 'I'm not putting it out in the shed beside the goats. It's staying by the fire; it's only a little baby.'

But, anyway, she won her way; the old woman kept her seal. Old John carried on as usual and old Mary carried on as usual, doing her jobs; and time passed by. But within three or four months the seal grew and it began to follow the old woman every place, every place the old woman went. It followed her to the shore and followed her back, just like a dog. It loved the old woman dearly. But the old man — he couldn't stand this seal, he hated it! He couldn't look at it.

Time passed by and in came the spring of the year. Now the seal was nearly full grown, and Mary loved this seal like she never loved anything else in her life. One evening they were both sitting at their supper when they heard a knock at the door.

Mary said, 'John, did I hear someone knocking at the door?'

'Yes,' he said, 'go and see who it is.'

So Mary goes to the door. She opened it and standing there was a young man in his twenties, a nice-looking young man in his twenties.

'Hello,' she says, 'young man. What is it? What can I do for you?'

'Well, ma'm,' he said, 'to tell you the truth, I came up from the village and they told me . . . I'm looking for a — a room to rent . . . and they told me in the village that sometimes you and your husband rent a room to people for two or three weeks in the summertime.'

'Yes,' she said, 'we do, we really do that. It's only both ourselves here, we stay — just me and my husband — we have no family of our own and we've got a large house; sometimes we do let a room. But don't let me have you standing in the doorway — come in!' So she took the young man in, to the kitchen fire.

She told old John, 'John, this is a young man here who has walked up from the village and he's wondering if we could rent him a room for a few weeks.'

'Well,' John says, 'I'm sure the spare room is never used very much by you and me, and if the young man is needing a room for a few weeks I don't see any harm in letting him have it.'

'By the way,' the old woman says, 'what is your name?'

'My name is Iain, and,' he said, 'I'm an artist. I've come to do some landscape painting and I would be very much obliged if you would let me have the room for a couple of weeks.'

'Fine,' the old man says.

She said, 'Would you like some supper?'

So the old woman told him how much she needed for the room, and the young man was quite pleased at what he had to pay, and she said, 'You can have your meals with us if you feel like it.'

'That'll do nicely,' the young man said. 'That'll just suit me fine. I won't be any trouble to you.'

But he never as much as glanced at the seal sitting in the basket by the fire! He never paid any attention to the seal; he just treated it as if it didn't exist. And the old woman thought this very queer. So while he was sitting down at the table having some supper with them the old woman looked at him, at the young man, and she thought she'd seen him someplace before. When she looked at his eyes she thought she'd seen those eyes somewhere before. But she racked her brains to think — who had she seen that he was like? He was like somebody but she couldn't remember. Anyway, with talking to him and the old man, the thought of his resemblance went out of her mind.

But the old man, old John, he and the young man got to talking and cracking, and they just made it off together like two peas. The old man started explaining to the young man, to young Iain, about his nets getting torn with the seals and how his fish were destroyed, how this affected his living and he's wishing that something would be done to get rid of some of the seals round the bay so's he could do more fishing.

And old Mary said, 'You're always getting down upon the poor seals. I'm sure they must have their time, too, they must live just the same as everybody else. But, anyway,' the old woman says, 'come and I'll show you your room.'

So she took the young man upstairs and showed him the room. He thanked her very much. 'That's very nice; that'll just suit me fine.'

But she noticed all he had was one small package under his arm: he didn't have any cases or anything . . . one package under his arm.

So they walked out on the landing and the young man said, 'I'll be bidding you both goodnight.'

She went down the stairs and they heard him shutting the door. Then all was quiet. Now, while the young man was in the bedroom, the seal got up out of the basket and started 'honk-honk-honk' round the floor.

The old man says, 'What's wrong with that animal?'

'Och, he's a wee bit excited tonight,' she said.

And the old woman sat and petted him. 'You're getting excited; I never saw you excited like that before.' But she managed to calm the seal and got him quietened. She and old John talked for a while and then went off to their bed.

The next morning they were at breakfast when the young man came down the stairs. He said to old John, 'You wouldn't mind if I were to go out with you, maybe sometime when you're — when I'm not painting — if it's too dull for painting — to watch you fishing?'

'O-oh, no,' he said, 'Iain! I'd be only too glad to have you along for company. In fact, did you ever row a boat before?'

'Well,' Iain said, 'I've never rowed a boat before, but I know how it's done. I believe I could learn quick enough.'

So after breakfast the old man took him down, he showed him the boat and some of the spare nets he had hung up on the sticks along the beach to dry. And he showed him all the holes that the seals had caused and some of the carcasses of fish he had thrown away that the seals had left. But the young man never said a thing.

He stayed there for a week. He had his meals in the house and he walked away every morning; some days he was away all day and sometimes he came back late at night.

But one night the old man said, 'You know, Iain, tomorrow I'm going to shift my nets farther round the beach to a place I've never fished or set a net before. And I wonder if you would come and give me a wee help?'

'Oh, certainly,' he said, 'I'd be willing to help you. In fact, I don't think I'll be doing very much tomorrow so I'll go with you, if you want me to!'

'I would like that very much,' the old man said.

To make a long story short, the next day after breakfast he said goodbye to the old woman — Iain treated the old woman casually, just casually. But he loved old John, he loved the old man. He would do anything and go anywhere with the old man, and the old man was the same way with him: at night-time when the young man was in his room the old man used to sit and talk to the old woman. 'My, such a nice young man, that! I wish we had a son like him; what a young, strong powerful man. And you want to see him rowing a boat!' The good things he would say about this young man to the old woman!

That morning he and the old man got ready to go away in the boat. He put a net in the back and they rowed away out, farther than John had ever been before, out in the bay.

The old man looks up. 'I hope it doesn't come rain, or wind.' And it got kind of dark.

The young man says, 'Maybe it's a storm going to blow up.'

The old man said, 'I hope not, because I don't want to have to come back out here tomorrow in rough weather.'

But no sooner were the words out of the old man's mouth than it started to rain, then the wind got up. And it came a storm! They were a good mile and a half away from the beach. The net was out. And it got so rough they could barely make their way back.

So the old man said to the young man, 'You take one oar and I'll take the other and we'll row as fast as we can.'

They rowed hard against the waves, but the waves got too rough and they were battling against the heavy waves when the boat overturned. The old man fell into the sea. And the young man fell into the sea.

He was shouting, 'Iain, Iain! This way, Iain, this way, Iain. Grab an oar, Iain, and try to keep yourself afloat, grab an oar and try to keep yourself afloat!'

The old man got hold of one of the wooden oars and he got it under his arm; he was swimming with one hand. But he looked all around for Iain . . . Iain was gone. And he swam on; he could see the land in the distance. He swam on and on till he was getting fairly exhausted — he knew he was never going to make it. He lost the grip on the oar and was just about sinking into the water when he felt this thing coming up under him. He put his hands out; he thought it was a bit of floating stick — and he felt — it was a big furry seal! It came right up under him and he put his two arms around its neck and away the seal went as fast as it could go. Right to the beach and the old man's clinging on to the seal, fairly exhausted clinging on to the seal.

So it swam right in, on to the beach till it couldn't go any farther with the weight of the old man, and the old man sprachled on his hands and knees and crawled up on to the shore where he flung himself down completely exhausted. The seal turned and went away.

By now the old woman's out, waiting and waiting and walking up and down the beach, looking to see, spying away out, looking to see if she could see the boat. But she couldn't see any boat. She never noticed that the old man was lying on his fours on the shingle on the tidemark with his feet in the water. After she walked along the beach a ways, though, she saw him. She pulled him up and asked him what happened. Oh, he was in a terrible state!

'Oh,' he said, 'Iain is gone. The storm caught us and the boat capsized and Iain is gone. We'll never see him again, he's gone!'

So the old woman oxtered him up to the house and made him take off his wet clothes and she put a blanket round him, put him sitting in the chair and gave him a drink of whisky. But all she could get out of his mouth was 'Iain is gone; we'll never

see Iain again'. Finally the old woman got him kind of settled
down. She asked him what happened.

He told her the tale ... 'I was finished, I was exhausted,
completely gone — only for a seal.'

She said, 'A seal!'

He said, 'A seal,' he said, 'saved my life!'

'How did it save your life?'

He said, 'It came up below me and I put my arms round it —
and would you believe it, Mary,' he said, 'after all the things
that I've said about these animals — it saved my life!'

'Well,' she said, 'it's good that it did you a good turn; maybe
now you'll change your mind about seals.'

He said, 'You know, from now on I'll never say another
angry word against a seal, because it's thanks to the seal my
life's been saved, been spared!'

After a while they went to bed. But the old man couldn't
rest, he tossed and turned all night. 'Tomorrow morning, Mary,'
he said, 'we'll have to go down to the village and notify the
policeman, tell him what happened to that young man.'

So, true to his word, the next morning the old man went
down to the local police station in the wee village and reported
the young man to the policeman — one constable that stayed
in the wee village. John walked over to the hotel and asked them
in the hotel if Iain had been staying there. And nobody — there
were only about a dozen houses in the village and the one
hotel — nobody had ever heard tell of the young man! Nobody
had ever seen him! He had never come to the village the whole
time he'd been with John and Mary. Nobody ever saw him
coming, nobody ever saw him going, nobody ever sent him up
to the old man and woman in the first place! It was a complete
mystery; nobody knew him.

So the old man walked home and he told the old woman. She
says, 'Somebody must have seen him somewhere about the
village when he came here first!'

'No,' he said, 'nobody saw him at all. It's a sheer mystery.'

Anyway, by the time the old man had got back and had sat
down for a cup of tea, the policeman had arrived with his bicycle
to have a talk to the old woman and the old man about this
missing young man. So the old man explained to him what

happened . . . they went out in the boat and the boat capsized and he swam to shore — but he never mentioned the seal, about the seal saving his life, to the policeman, never mentioned it.

Well, the policeman took all the particulars he could. 'Now,' he said, 'how long had he been here?'

'Well,' the old man said, 'he'd been here, he was with us for about ten days . . . such a nice boy, too, such a beautiful young man and such a handsome young man. We got on so well together, he was just like a son to me. And I'm going to miss him terribly.'

The policeman looked — the seal was sitting in the basket. 'My, Mary,' he said, 'your seal is fairly growing!'

'Aye,' she said, 'it's fairly growing; he's getting a wee bit too big. It's about time he was going back to the sea.'

So, the policeman asked, 'Did he have any identification or anything about him — where did Iain stay?'

She said, 'He stayed up in the bedroom, the spare room up the stairs,' she said.

'Well, you don't mind', the policeman said, 'if I go up and see, have a look through his papers and things? Maybe I'll get the address of his parents or his family or something. Then we'll know where he came from, for a report to his people that he's a-missing.'

'All right,' say the old man and woman.

So the old man and the woman and the policeman walked up the stairs, the old woman opened the bedroom door. And they walked in. They looked around — the bed was made the same way as the old woman had made it when she made it the first time — it never was slept on. There were no cases, there were no parcels, there was nothing! In the room — not one single thing — except over in the far corner next to the window was a picture-frame, a canvas picture framed. The back of it was turned to the old man and the old woman, the front facing the window. And the old man walked over.

He says, 'This is what he's been working on the whole time.' And he turned it round, he looked at it and stepped back — the old man gasped.

The policeman said, 'What is it, John?'

14

'Well,' he said, 'it's this picture . . . Would you come here and see this, Mary!'

'What is it?' she said. 'What is —? What has he been drawing? He said he was an artist.'

'Yes, he's an artist; he was an artist,' he said, 'poor boy. He was an artist all right, and a good one, too!'

They turned the picture round: there was the most beautiful picture you'd ever seen in your life. The picture of an old woman gathering dulse on the shore — old Mary the way she was, exactly as if you were looking at the old woman herself, picking up a baby seal from among the dulse — was the picture Iain had made. And the policeman was amazed but old Mary never said a word.

John said, 'Mary, how did he manage to paint that?'

'Och,' she said, 'I told him the story, he probably painted it from memory.'

So the policeman says, 'Well, there's little we can do about it.'

But time passed by and there never was another word about the man, young Iain's body never was found. About a week after that, the old man and woman carried the seal down to the shore, put it back in the tide and away the seal went. But there was never another word about Iain and the old man never again complained about seals. And whenever the old woman went down to gather her seaweed along the shore she would look out and see the seals in the bay floating about; she would give a wee smile to herself and say, 'Well, Iain, you've finally proved your point!' She knew he'd been a silkie.

SHELL HOUSE

I happened to be in the village of Clachan in Argyllshire in 1941, when I'd left home at the age of thirteen and travelled down the west coast of Kintyre. And I got a little work with an old man called John MacDougall in Dunscaig Farm beside Clachan. He lived with his wife and his maid, and he had a couple of sisters who lived in the village. I got a couple of weeks employment with him. I was sleeping, staying in the barn, and I worked with John. I respected the old man very much. He's long gone dead now. Maybe some of his relations are still around. And one evening I was sitting in an old corn kist. I had a little bed in the barn where I stayed. John came in and we sat there and talked for a while. I was telling him about my search for stories. 'Well,' he said, 'there's some stories I've heard myself.' I said, 'John, if I were to tell you a story, would you tell me a story?' 'Well,' he said, 'I've never told any stories, Duncan, but this is one that my grandmother used to tell a long time ago. When me and my little sisters were very small we used to listen to our grandmother telling a story.' And this is the story he told me.

IN A LITTLE VILLAGE a long time ago on the West Coast there once lived a young woman called Margaret MacKay. Margaret MacKay's father was the local grave digger. In his spare time he was a beadle of the church, pulling the bell and taking care of the church. And Margaret's mother had died when she was very small. She attended the local village school. And of course Margaret spent most of her time — because the cottage that they lived in was beside the sea — her love was collecting shells. She spent every spare moment she could find collecting all those beautiful shells. Shells of all descriptions, of all the little creatures she could find. And of course she placed them around her house. It was known to the local villagers as Shell House. The people knew Margaret's obsession for shells. When they came for a visit, they had to walk down an old rough road leading from the local village to the house by the seaside where Margaret lived with her father. And Margaret would spend many evenings along the beach that stretched for miles. There were many beautiful coves in the bay where she would wander while her daddy was taking care of the graveyard and looking after the church.

Margaret was very happy. But the happiness in her life was taking care of her shells. Even though her father was a grave-digger, they kept a large amount of ducks and hens. That was all the animals they had, only ducks and hens. And Margaret took care of them. But then, when she was in her twenties, her father died and left her all alone. Of course Margaret continued to carry on with her life as usual. She lived all alone, but would bring her eggs to the village. She would take them to the local store.

Now in the local store was a man named Angus MacDonald. Angus had been in school with Margaret. And his father had died when Angus was very small. But Angus' mother was still alive. And Angus' mother had a great love for Margaret. She loved her! And she was always telling Angus.

'Angus,' she said, 'such a wonderful young woman! Angus, how could you not marry her?'

And he would say, 'Mother, of course, why should I marry the young woman? We were in school together, and she has no affection, no love for me. We are just good friends!'

Now the thing about Angus, he lived with his mother in this small village — he ran the local post office in the local store where the people came for their little groceries — but Angus was kind of mean. He loved money, was very fond of it. He went out of his way to make a penny, or make a shilling. And each day after he closed the store — he had a little house attached to the post office — he would make his mother a cup of tea. She was a very old woman was Angus' mother. And everything she brought up in the conversation was about Margaret, Margaret MacKay.

'Angus, she's such a beautiful woman. Why don't you and her get closer?'

'Mother, she's just a good friend of mine. And of course you can't go and ask a young lady to marry you or something!'

Now the village was not very large. The local villagers knew all about Angus' mother's obsession for Margaret. But not so with Angus MacDonald! As far as he was concerned, Margaret was only his good friend, his school mate. But anyhow, not far from the village was a large house where a laird lived who owned most of the village and the land all around. And Angus would always take eggs to the big house. But it happened Angus would try his best to skin a fly for a penny, as we call it on the West Coast! Because Angus was greedy. He never helped anyone in the village of any kind. I mean, the old folk were poor. He would just try and cheat them as much as he could. But his mother was an old darling lady. And of course everyone knew her. But she didn't come out very much. Here my story begins.

Two days, three days, passed and Margaret never turned up at the store. And Angus was completely out of eggs when he got a message from the big house, the laird's house on the hill. They were having some kind of party, some kind of birthday meeting together, and they needed some eggs. Now it was late in the evening when word arrived. And the eggs were badly needed at the big house.

So Angus said, 'Mother, I've had a message from the big house. I'll have to walk down to Margaret's tonight to see if she has any eggs. I can walk down myself.' Now it was about a mile down the old rough track leading to the beach and Margaret's cottage, surrounded by shells.

'Well,' she said, 'it's a very cold night. Take your coat with you.'

'Och no, Mother,' he said, 'I'll not need a coat. I'll just take my scarf.' He wrapped the scarf round his neck. And he walked down. The road was not very good and not used for anything. Vehicles could never go down the road that led to Margaret's house. And as he came down — he had not come to Margaret's house very often, but he'd been there once or twice — he saw that the house, every single window of the house was lighted. Angus thought this was very strange. Because Margaret had only kept one little room lit, one light on in the kitchen when he'd visited her previously. But tonight the house was in a lunary of lights. It was paraffin lamps. And Angus came up. Now there was a large bay window that faced the shore. This was the kitchen area.

And when Angus came along, he looked in through the window. The curtains were parted. And there to his amazement he could see a large number of people sitting with Margaret. Margaret was in the middle and she was busy talking away. Angus stood for a few minutes. And he thought to himself, 'Who could this be? Where did these people come from?' And then he remembered . . . maybe it's tinkers. 'Maybe it's tinkers,' he said. Margaret always catered for the local tinkers when they came through the village. She always gave them eggs and was very good to them. But Angus said, 'I've never seen any tinkers in the village for a while. It can't be tinkers.' So he went up to the door and he knocked. And he waited. Then Margaret came to the door.

She says, 'Hello, Angus, what is it?'

He says, 'Margaret, excuse me for bothering you. But I've just got word from the big house — I'm needing some eggs.'

'Oh,' she said, 'I see. But I was so busy that I couldn't get up with the eggs. I've got plenty.'

'Well,' he said, 'I'm needing about three dozen for the big house. Margaret, who's all the people?'

'Och,' she said, 'Angus, it's some friends of mine.'

'Friends, Margaret?' he said. 'What . . . are they local tinkers or something?'

'No, no, Angus,' she said, 'it's no tinkers at all. It's some friends.'

'But,' he says, 'Margaret, where did . . . are they from the village?'

'No, no, Angus,' she said, 'they're not from the village. They're just some friends of mine.' And because the wind was blowing it was very cold. And she couldn't have him standing at the door, she said, 'Angus, you'd better come in.' She brought him into the little kitchen in the house. And sitting around were about fifteen people. Angus looked all around. But Margaret had gone in before him. And as he closed the door behind he felt something soft hanging on the back of the door. A coat, a beautiful coat, it felt so soft. Angus closed the door without using the handle. He just pushed it. And there was the long, soft coat hanging behind the door. Angus' hand sank into the coat.

When he walked into the room Margaret said, 'Excuse me, friends, but we have a visitor.' And all these people looked up. Angus looked. He saw the strangest set of people he ever saw in his life. Because everyone looked identical. They were all round faced . . . wonderful looking people. And they all had these beautiful brown eyes. And Margaret was saying, 'Excuse me, friends, but my visitor has come to call. I'm sorry.'

'Oh,' one of the men sitting in the corner says, 'you've no need to be sorry, Margaret. Any friend of yours is a friend of ours.' And he stood up and Angus could see that everyone was dressed in a long coat, the same identical coat. Everyone was dressed the same way. And the one who stood, the largest one said, 'Welcome, friend!' And Angus shook hands with him.

He says, 'I'm Angus MacDonald from the village and I've come for some eggs.'

'Oh,' he said, 'don't let us interfere with you.'

'Oh,' he says, 'it's no problem.'

He says, 'You'd better sit down then and rest yourself.'

Margaret said, 'I'll go and get you your eggs, Angus.' And she filled a basket.

Angus looked around. There were young people, there were old people. There were people middle-aged. About fifteen of them.

21

Then Margaret came forward and she said, 'Angus, I'm sorry. But you could stay!'

'Oh no,' he said, 'I can't stay, Margaret. I'm really sorry. I've got to hurry back because the laird in the big house needs his eggs.' He said, 'I'm sorry, people, but I have to go.' Not one spoke except this particular man.

He stood up and said, 'Angus, you're walking home to the village tonight. It's kind of cold. Take my coat.'

'Oh,' Angus said, 'I could not take your coat.'

'Yes,' he said, 'Angus, please take my coat! You're a friend of Margaret's, you're a friend of mine!' And he took off his coat. He held it open. 'Now it's a long, cold way home. Put this on you!'

And Angus said, 'Well, I thank you very much. In a little while I'll return it.'

'Oh no,' he says, 'don't return it to me. You keep it! I have another.'

Angus slipped into this coat. It was warm and comfortable and went down to his heels. It felt like fur but it was not fur. It was the strangest coat. But when Angus put it on, he felt very strange . . . he felt his heart light. His heart became light. He wanted to stay with these people. 'Who were these people?' thought Angus.

And then Margaret came in with the basket of eggs and she said, 'Here you are, Angus! Will I see you again?'

'Well,' he says, 'I'll see you tomorrow maybe, Margaret. Good night, Margaret. I'm sorry for interrupting your friends.'

'Oh, Angus,' she says, 'don't you worry.'

But he says, 'Margaret, will you tell me, are they tinkers?'

'No, no, no,' she says, 'Angus, they're not tinkers. They're my friends.'

But he says, 'Where have they come from?'

She says, 'Angus, I have to tell you. But will you promise me faithfully?'

'Margaret,' he said, 'you know you and I have been in school with each other, together. I promise you anything within reason.'

'Angus,' she said, 'will you promise you will never tell a soul as long as you live? Have I got your promise?'

'Margaret,' he said, 'you and I've been friends since our child-hood. I promise you anything!'

She says, 'Angus, they're seal people.'

'Ach,' he said, 'Margaret, there's no such a thing as seal people!'

'Yes, Angus,' she says, 'there are seal people. They're my friends, and they've come for a visit.'

'But, Margaret,' he said, 'they all look alike!'

'Yes,' she said, 'they all look alike. And they're my friends. But anyhow, Angus, I'll maybe see you tomorrow if I have time.'

'But, Margaret,' he said, 'there's no such a thing as seal people!'

'Angus,' she said, 'now listen to me carefully. One of them has given you his coat. You take care of that coat! Look after it. And you will feel better with it.'

Angus walked away with his basket of eggs. Angus walked home with the basket in his hand. And he was whistling to himself. He felt comfortable. He felt strange. He felt happy. Some kind of lightness had went to his heart. And he was thinking mostly of Margaret. 'Such a wonderful woman,' he thought. 'My mother is right. She is a beautiful lady.' And when he walked home to the little store where he lived with his mother, he went in and put the eggs on the table. His mother was sitting knitting by the fireside on her old rocking chair. And she looked up.

She said, 'Angus, you're back.'

'Yes, Mother,' he said, 'I'm back.'

'Did you get the eggs from Margaret? How was she?'

'Oh,' he says, 'Margaret . . . Mother, she's fine.'

And then she said, 'Angus, where did you get the coat?'

He says, 'Mother, I borrowed it from —' now he didn't want to tell. He said, 'I borrowed it from Margaret. It must have been her father's.'

She says, 'No, Angus, that's not her father's coat. You're taller than her father. I knew old John well. But he never had a coat like that in all his time. That's a . . . come over closer to me till I feel it.' And he walked over, and the old woman reached

23

over and she groped it with her hand. She said, 'Angus, that's the most beautiful thing I've ever seen! Where did you get it?'

He said, 'I borrowed it from Margaret. Because it was kind of cold when I left the house.'

'And how is the dear girl?'

'Oh,' he said, 'she's fine!'

She said, 'Angus, wouldn't she make a wonderful wife?'

'Och, Mother,' he said, 'of course she'd make a wonderful wife. But she doesn't want anything to do with me!'

'Angus,' she said, 'it's the only thing that would make me happy — if you and Margaret were to get together. Because I'll not be with you for very long, you know. I'm getting old and my time is nearly come.'

'Ach, Mother,' he said, 'behave yourself!' But he started to sing in the house! And his old mother's looking.

And she said, 'Angus, what's come over you?'

'Och, Mother,' he said, 'I feel fine tonight.'

She says, 'Angus, I think I know what's happened to you. You're in love!'

'Well, Mother, maybe I am,' he said.

So he took his coat off and he hung it behind the door. But from that moment on Angus became a changed man. Margaret visited the old woman, because she visited Angus' mother at least once a week. She would sit and have a cup of tea with Angus' mother.

But Angus' mother's only thing was — 'And what do you think of Angus now then? Isn't he a handsome . . . '

'Ach,' she said, 'Angus is fine. He's a good friend of mine.'

But Angus became a changed man. And because Angus changed within a few days, Margaret began to see this in him. He was happy! He was whistling. He was singing. He was serving the store. And then Margaret began to hear after she returned to her cottage what wonderful work Angus was doing for the old people in the village. He was helping everyone. He was good to everyone. And one day Angus put on his coat and he walked down to Margaret's house. When he came to Margaret's house she was busy washing eggs. You know eggs get dirty sometimes? She was washing them. And he had his coat on. He was smiling, whistling to himself.

24

He says, 'Margaret, I've come to ask you a question.'

She says, 'Yes, Angus?'

He said, 'Would you care to walk with me?' And he had his long coat on.

'Where would you like to walk, Angus?' she said.

He said, 'I would like to walk along the beach.'

'Well,' she said, 'wait and I'll get my coat.' And Margaret went behind the door, and she took down the coat. The very coat that he'd put his hand against when he'd felt it — identical to the one that he owned, that was given to him. She says, 'Angus, do you like your coat?'

'Oh, Margaret, I love my coat! But I love something more than my coat. I love you, Margaret! Margaret,' he said, 'would you marry me?'

'Well, Angus,' she said, 'I've been waiting for that for a long, long time.'

He said, 'Have you?'

'Of course, Angus,' she said. 'You're not the same person.'

'No, Margaret,' he said, 'I'm not the same person I was a long time ago. I think I'm in love.' (And I swear over my mother's grave as he sat there back in 1941 I can see him smiling, old John MacDougall's face as he sat there. He was probably thinking of his own love in years.) And as they walked along the beach he asked her again, would she marry him?

She says, 'Yes, I've been waiting for that for a long time.' But anyhow, they came home and they sat and they talked. Margaret had promised she would marry Angus MacDonald. So, to make a long story short, there was a small wedding in the village. Everyone in the village was interested and excited. Angus Mac-Donald was marrying Margaret MacKay in the village church. Of course, the local minister was there. And everybody wanted to see the beautiful bride dressed for the occasion.

Everyone turned up at the church who was invited. But to the amazement of everyone, Angus and Margaret appeared in two long coats at the church. Two long, black coats down to their feet. And everyone gazed and stared. Where were the beautifully dressed bride and groom? But they could see the faces of Angus and Margaret were blossoming in happiness. Just dressed as they were. There was a small, quiet wedding and

Angus and Margaret were married. A small reception in the village, and everyone turned up. But to the amazement of everyone, Angus and Margaret wouldn't take off their coats, for no one breathing!

So, a few days later Angus got a young man to run the store for him. And he went to live with Margaret in her little cottage by the seaside. And of course his old mother, she was just over the moon, over the moon! This is what she wanted all her life. Now she could die in peace. So everyone was wondering, even the local minister, why Margaret and Angus were so happy. Why hadn't they dressed for a great wedding in the church?

But anyhow, within a few weeks Angus' mother died. There was a great sermon. And to the amazement of everyone, Angus and Margaret turned up to the sermon dressed in their long coats as usual. And this of course made the local villagers think again about the change that came over Angus MacDonald. For Angus was happy — he was the happiest man of all. And three weeks after his mother had died he sold the store to the local man who had run it for him. And he and Margaret lived happily in their little cottage by the shore. But sometimes Margaret would hire a young man to take care of her hens and her ducks for her. Because they would go off on a journey to visit friends. They were gone for many weeks. And people often wondered where Margaret and Angus had gone. Because no one knew exactly who their friends were.

And they would say, 'I wonder when Angus and Margaret will be coming back again?'

Whenever they appeared in the village they always appeared in their long coats. Whenever they walked along the beach, they always appeared in long coats. And Angus and Margaret didn't have any children. They lived very happily in the little shell house till their old age. In her late seventies Margaret died. The local minister was a dear friend of theirs.

When Angus came to him he said, 'Minister, when I die bury me beside Margaret. And there's Margaret's coat; and you'll get mine when I die.' So after a few years Angus finally died. And of course the minister kept his promise, he would bury Angus' coat with him as he had done with Margaret's. But then for some strange reason, before the funeral service for Angus, he took down the coat from a peg where it hung. And he put his hand in the pocket. He brought out a little red book. And he sat down and he looked at it.

He said, 'This is very strange. This is a strange, strange story.' And the minister read the story from the little red book that was found in Angus' pocket. And Angus was buried beside his wife with his coat. And the minister kept the little book, and learned the story. And old John MacDougall told me, the local minister told this story to his grandmother. And that's how he came to know it. So I'm telling it to you, and that's how you've come to know it.

SILKIE'S REVENGE

This story was told to me by Neil MacCallum, a stone-dyke mason of a crofting family, many years ago. His forbears had come from some of the islands in the Hebrides and this was one of his favourites. There are many stories about silkies that take in every type of person — farmers, shepherds, policemen — and, like this one, a minister. It's supposed to have been true ...

NOW MANY YEARS AGO in a wee village on the West Coast there lived a minister. He hadn't a very big parish. Houses in these days were kind o' thinly scattered. He didn't have a big congregation coming to his church, so he had a lot of time to spend to himself. Mostly all ministers in these days kept a boat for to do a bit o' fishing in their spare time. And having his manse by the shoreside, he had a boat and did a bit o' fishing, but he also had a net that he set sometimes for fish. And he used to give a lot of fish away to the people of the village who weren't able to fish for themselves. He was quite happily married with his wife and one wee girl. But he had a terrible anger against the seals — because these nets were very hard to get and it cost a lot of money to buy one — every morning when he went down he found holes in his net, some of his fish were eaten and destroyed. Even though he was the minister, he swore revenge on the seals.

On Sunday mornings before he went to church, he always used to go down and lift his net early before the tide went out so the gulls wouldn't go near his fish. He went down to the net one Sunday morning early and there caught was a wee baby seal — it wasn't very old, maybe a week and no more. It was still alive! And the funny thing — not a fish was touched in his net, there was a lot of fish in the net.

But he took the wee baby seal by the flipper. 'You little rascal!' he said. 'You'll grow up some day to be a big seal and then you'll destroy my net if I'm still here.' And he took the wee baby seal, hit its head against a rock, and threw it among the seaweed on the shore. He turned round to take pieces of seaweed out of his net, and he looked out. About ten or fourteen feet out in the sea was a seal and its head was up out of the water — it was watching him. He shook his fist at it. And it disappeared in the water.

So he walked home with his fish to his wife and told her about his net and all his hate for the seals.

His wife, she was a gentle kind o' cratur. 'You know,' she told him, 'you should try and leave the seals alone. They're entitled to have as much fish oot o' the sea as what you have.'

He said, 'You can say what you like but I hate these creatures, you'll never get me to like them in any way.'

So a few months later, the end of summer, his wife became very sick and they sent for the doctor. The doctor tried everything in the world to save her, but she just pined away and died. And the minister was very very upset. That period of time he never set a net or did any fishing; all his time was spent looking after his wee lassie Morag, who was only four years old.

But between doing his service in the church, doing his garden and his housework, he didn't have enough time left for the wee lassie, his boat, and his net. He advertised in a local newspaper for a housekeeper, which usually they did in these days when there was too much to do.

About a week passed and one day he and his little girl were sitting at their wee bit o' supper when a knock came to the door.

And the wee lassie said, 'Daddy, I'll go and see who it is.'

He thought it was some o' the folk from the village or something. The wee girl went to the door and there stood this woman in her mid-thirties. Her father shouted to her, 'Who is it, Morag?'

She said, 'It's a lady, Daddy.'

So the minister came walking out to the door and he said to this young woman, 'Hello, what can I do for you?'

She said, 'I saw your advertisement in the local newspaper, you're looking for a housekeeper.'

'Yes,' he said, 'I am.'

'Well,' she said, 'I've come about the job.'

'Well,' he said, 'don't stand there at the door, come in!' So he took her into the house, asked her her name, where she came from.

She said she was a widow and her name was Selina.

'Look, you can stay in the house,' he said, and he told her how much he was going to pay her. 'The main purpose I want you for is to take care o' my little daughter because I havena much time, with my garden and my fishin, and,' he said, 'the child's mother has passed away.'

'I'll take good care of her,' she said.

So they agreed on a wage for her and he showed her where to stay, her bedroom, and she said that was all right.

'Now,' he said, 'ye can have your meals in the kitchen with me whenever you need to.'

So he took a good look at her: she had long dark hair and brown eyes, a good-looking young woman she was, very quiet. But the moment the wee lassie saw her, wee Morag just took to her right away. She was a weak kind o' wee lassie, Morag, and the minister was quite happy.

So she was there for about two weeks and everywhere she went, Morag went with her. It was just like a second mother to her. The minister never paid attention for the first two or three weeks; he just thought it was the affection of the wee lassie after losing her mother — why she was clinging to this woman. And this Selina just loved this wee lassie, took her everywhere. During the evening when the minister was in his room doing his work for the church, writing his papers, learning his sermon and that, Selina would take wee Morag away with her along the beach and the minister thought nothing of it. And they would be gone for hours. And when she came back Morag seemed a happier and more radiant child than ever she was in her life. The minister was very pleased.

So she was there for about two months . . . whenever the wee girl came into the house and her daddy wanted to speak to her, it was just 'Selina this' and 'Selina that.' She just sat in Selina's lap and cuddled her and the minister thought it kind of queer that she should think so much of her, you see. So even at mealtime, when they sat down to have their meal together, the two of them would just pick at their food, they wouldn't hardly eat anything. And this upset the minister too.

So as time went by he began to get really upset and he turned round and said to her, 'Look, can we not have a decent meal together sometime?' And they were always so quiet, they couldn't wait till the meal was over till they got away on the beach. 'Where do youse go every evening?' he said, 'why do youse go, how do youse spend so much time on the beach — cold or wind or any day, you always go on the beach — can you not find comfort in here, in the manse with a good fire?'

'Morag loves to swim and,' she said, 'I always like to take her to the beach, we enjoy the beach together so much.'

But another month passed by and the minister began to see

that the lassie was slowly going away from him, clinging to this woman. So he made his mind up that he was going to either tell her off or give her the sack, or he was going to have a settlement with her. He made up his mind the next morning . . . he's going to take them fishing.

Now you know these wee rowing boats, there's a seat in the middle, a seat up in the front, and a seat across the back. The minister took his fishing rod and he said to Selina and Morag, 'I want youse today to come fishin with me.' So they went out fishing. And the minister's sitting rowing in the front of the boat with his rod in the bow, when he comes out just about where he'd seen the seal when he'd lifted his net that one Sunday morning — it wasn't far out from the beach. And Selina was sitting at the back of the boat, her arm round wee Morag's neck, and Morag and her were whispering to each other. This upset the minister so much.

'Look,' he said to Selina, 'what are ye tryin tae do to me; are you trying tae take my little girl from me, only thing I have left in this world now my wife is gone? I've been good to ye and I treated ye right in this place and I've let you do what you like. But now it's getting unbearable. I need Morag as much as you need her — in fact I prob'ly need her more. After all,' he said, 'she's my daughter, not yours! You're just tryin to take the only thing from me that I really love in this world.'

And Selina turned round. 'And you done the same for me!'

'Woman,' he said, 'I did nothing for you.'

She said, 'Look, you took the only thing that *I* really loved in this world, ye took my baby and hit its head against a stone!'

And the minister just stood aghast — he didn't know what to say, when Selina put her arm round Morag's neck and both of them went over the back of the boat and disappeared in the water. The bubbles came up and they were gone. From that day on, till the day he died, the minister never saw his daughter or Selina again.

SALTIE THE SILKIE

This travelling family was unique because instead of walking on the road they sailed on the sea, and people called them 'sea tinkers.' I heard my father a long time ago speaking about them — there's only supposed to have been one travelling family that sailed, were sea tinkers, I think they were MacAlisters. My old grandfather, he'd remembered them ... they used to sail through the Crinan Canal, right down, right round all the coast, all the islands; this great old clinkerbuilt boat they had. Aye, he told me the ruins of that boat lay on the shore for years and years and years, till it melted away.

IT WAS THIS MAN, his wife, and two grown-up sons. The couple had married very young and bought this old boat. The man sailed from island to island and he kept to the coastline — very very seldom he ever was on the road except maybe he would pitch his tent and stay at the shoreside in the winter months when it was too rough to sail. But otherwise his wife and him and his two sons always stayed in the water with the boat . . . it was a good size o' boat, and it took three folk to handle it, like the father and the two sons.

So one day the mother, who wasn't too old a woman even though she had grown-up sons, had a wee girl, a baby. And it was only a couple of days old when it died. Naturally in these days the travelling folk didn't register the weans as they do nowadays; they just went and had a wee ceremony, buried it by the shoreside. And the woman was very very sad at losing her baby — she always wanted a wee girl — she was so upset.

So they had their wee sermon as travelling folk really do, packed their tent stuff in the boat, and away they sailed. They sailed along slowly, the boys were rowing the boat and the old man was taking a rest up in the front, the woman sitting at the back. They were sailing along quite naturally when the woman looked over the back of the boat — there coming towards them was a wee baby seal, it was sailing along in the tide quite close behind the boat. So she reached out, lifted it in, and saw it was only about two or three days old. And the man saw her lifting it.

He said, 'Woman, what are ye gaunna do wi that?'

'It's a wee baby seal,' she said, 'it's lost. It's pro'bly lost its mother.'

'Well, put it back,' he said, 'in the water.'

'No,' she said, 'I'm gaunna keep it for a pet.'

So after her losing a baby the man didn't want to upset her too much. 'But, wumman,' he said, 'it'll mebbe be days before we come to a fairm or a croft along the shoreside afore ye can get milk for it. And it'll die wi ye anyway.'

She says, 'I've got plenty of milk — o' my own.' The woman was after losing her baby and she had plenty of milk in her own breasts.

'Ye canna do that,' the man says to his wife.

She says, 'I'm gaunnae dae it, and I'm keepin it for a pet.'

So, not to disturb her anymore, 'Well,' he says, 'please yoursel. But if onything bad happens tae ye ower the heid o' it, blame yoursel. Ye ken what these kind o' beasts is.' He said, 'Woman, that's no a wean, that's a seal.'

She says, 'I know it's a seal, it's a baby seal. And I'm takin it and I'm keepin it! I'm gaunna feed it.' So she turned her back to her man and her two sons, she held the baby to her breast and suckled the baby seal. So it was quite contented after having a good drink, it went to sleep. She rolled it in a shawl and she put it in her oxter like a baby.

So that night they docked their boat on the shoreside, and the man put up his tent as usual. The two sons went and got plenty of firewood and went for water, did everything that they needed done. She said nothing, she sat on a rock with the baby seal rolled in a shawl.

And her man came to her. 'Woman, look,' he said, 'I know that you lost your baby and I'm sorry for ye, but you're jist makkin too much o' that animal.'

She said, 'It's my animal and it's my pet and I'm gaunna keep it.'

So she kept it, she fed it and took care of it, looked after it. She had the seal for two or three months and the seal grew up, became a young pup and followed her every place she went. Naturally, when the man got accustomed to the seal and saw it was all right, he paid no more attention to it. And the two sons liked it as much as their mother liked it, but it wouldn't have anything to do with them, never came near them. It wouldn't go near the man either, but it loved the woman just like a pup.

Well they sailed round all the coast, they made baskets, made tin, and they hawked the houses. Wherever she went, the seal went with her, she wouldn't leave it any place. At night-time she used to take it down to the sea and teach it, put it in the water and it would go away swimming, it would play itself in the water and it always came back to her. Well, she had that seal for about six months — it was nearly half grown — till she couldn't hardly lift it, it was getting that big. Now it could go and fend for itself in the sea, and it always came back to her.

So one evening, it was the middle of summer and a lovely

evening, they docked their boat on the shoreside. And the old man and the laddies put up the tent. The woman thought she'd take down her seal to the shore as usual, it having been in the boat all day, and give it a swim. So she took it down, put it in the water, and away the seal went. It swam away out, it swam out — she kept shouting to it but it wouldn't come back — and then it disappeared. She waited and she waited, she waited for hours and she shouted and waited, but the seal never came back. It disappeared. She went back up to the tent, couldn't rest, she couldn't do anything she was so worried about her seal. She told her man about it.

'Ach, woman,' he said, 'it pro'bly got fed up wi yese, mebbe it's away back tae its ain folk anyway.' That's what he said, 'back tae its ain folk.'

So even the laddies tried to tell their mother. 'Look, Mother, ye canna keep it onyway, because someday when it gets too big it has to go away, it's got to take care o' itsel! Ye've done the best ye could for it, reared it up noo to take care o' itsel, so the best thing you could do is let it go.'

But this wouldn't content the old woman. After teatime she went back down again to the shoreside, and she had a good wee bit to walk from where the camp was to the shore where she'd put the seal. You could see the smoke of the camp but you couldn't see the camp. But when she came down to where she'd put the seal away, there sitting on the rock was the bonniest wee lassie she'd ever seen in her life — about eight or nine years old! She was sitting with her bare feet, dabbling with her feet in the water.

The woman went up and she said, 'Hello, dearie, where do you come fae?'

'Och,' she says, 'I cam away a long way.'

'But I've never seen any houses or any crofts,' the woman said to her, 'or any farms along the shore.'

'No, no, I cam a long way from here,' she says, 'a way along the shore.'

'And,' she says, 'what are you doin?'

'Och, I'm just playin mysel.' She says, 'Where do you come fae?'

'Oh,' she says, 'me and my husband and the two boys has got a tent along there, we have a boat and we sail on the sea.'

She said, 'Could I see your tent?'

The old woman said, 'What's about your people, your parents? Do they no miss ye, will they no come looking for ye?'

'No! No, they'll no come looking for me,' she said, 'I dinna have any parents, I'm an orphan.'

The old woman thought it was kind o' queer. She said, 'Are ye hungry?'

'Yes,' she said, 'I'm a wee bit hungry, a wee bit.'

'Well, come on up to wir fire,' she said, 'and I'll get ye something to eat. I'll try and get my boys to walk ye home tae where yir people is.'

But the wee lassie said, 'They cannae walk me home tae my people because my people is miles from here, I don't even know where my people is.'

So she took her up to the fire and she told the old man and the two laddies.

The old man was surprised when she came up with this wee lassie. 'But, wumman, whaur did ye get the wee lassie?' He said, 'You cannae take —'

'I got the wee lassie sittin on a rock,' she says, 'at the beach where my seal went awa. I went doon callin on the seal and it never cam back, I got this wee lassie sittin on the rock.'

The old man spoke to her in cant: '*Shanness, woman, that's hantle's wee kinchen*. Ten chances tae one, her faither's a shepherd or a fairmer along there,' and he said they would come looking for her. 'And,' he says, 'we'll get the blame for takkin her awa. Now we'll get intae trouble — we dinnae want to get intae trouble with the *country hantle*!'

The old woman said, 'The wee lassie's hungry. She's awfae hungry, gie her something to eat.'

So they gave her tea and cakes or bannocks, whatever kind of food they had. The wee lassie was quite content.

And the old woman says, 'Dearie, could my boys walk ye home and see that ye'll be safe?'

She says, 'I don't have any home! I've nowhere to go to, I don't know how I havena got nae home.'

The old *gadgie* says, 'Mebbe the wee *gurie's* wandert,' meaning 'maybe she's lost.' He spoke in cant to the woman so's the wee lassie wouldn't understand what he was saying.

But no, the wee lassie said, 'I would like to stay with youse and I would like to go sailin on your boat, I'd love to go sailin.'

Now the old woman liked this wee lassie. She said to her man, 'If she hasna got nae *hantle* belongin tae her, mebbe a wee orphan lassie, mebbe we could *bing* her wi us.'

'Oh no, *shanness*,' the old man said, 'you cannae dae that! Ye canna *bing* the wee lassie, bring the country folk's wee lassie wi ye, no way can you bring the wee lassie wi ye!'

But anyway, the wee lassie wanted to stay, there was no way they could convince her: she had no place to go.

Now, by the time they were finished talking it over, it was getting dark. The old woman had her own bed in the tent and she said, 'Dearie, ye canna go home the night, come in wi me.' So the old woman took the wee lassie in with her in bed; she slept beside the old woman all night till the morning.

They got up in the morning, had their wee bit breakfast, and the old man said to the wee lassie, 'Dearie, we'll have tae be movin on, we cannae stay here because there's nothing for us here. You sure we cannae take ye . . . ?'

'No,' she said, 'there's no place I want tae go tae except I want to go wi Mother.'

'But, dear,' he said, 'that's no your mother, ye must have a mother o' your own.'

'No, I don't have a mother,' she says, 'this is all the mother I have and this is all the mother I want!'

They tried to coax her and convince her, but no way. Anyway, by the time they got the boat ready and all their stuff packed into it, the wee lassie jumped in the boat with them.

Away she went with them, and the old woman said, 'I'm gaunnae keep her for the wean that I never had in my life, for the lassie I never had — I'm gaunnae keep her.'

The old man said, 'You're gaunnae get intae trouble, the police'll be after hus, the people'll be lookin for her all over the world and she'll be reported missin and we'll get the blame for stealin her!'

'Tsst,' the old woman said, 'look, if the police comes and we take good care o' her, we'll give her back and tell them we got

40

her on the beach miles away fae onybody — we thought she was lost and we dinna ken where her folk is.'

'Well,' the man said, 'I'm gaunnae hand her in to the first place I come tae.'

'Well,' the old woman said, 'okay, we'll dae that.'

But they took the wee lassie with them and they sailed from place to place, and from place to place for about six months; there was no word wherever they went to. And the wee lassie loved this old woman like she never loved anybody in her life — she wouldn't even go out of her sight! Wherever the old woman went, the lassie went with her. And the old woman loved this wee lassie like nothing on this earth.

Now this upset the two laddies because the woman had more affection for the wee lassie than she had for them, you see! But the lassie never paid any attention to the man and the laddies, she cracked to them and was civil but she never had any time for them.

So when they came beached at night, the old woman said to the wee lassie, 'Can you swim?'

'Well, Mother,' she says, 'I cannae swim but would you teach me?'

So that night after they'd beached the boat on the shoreside, she took the wee lassie well away from the camping place to a nice wee bit on the beach and took her in the water, and showed her what to do — move her hands and kick her feet, showed her how to swim. But she saw that the wee lassie could do it far better than she could tell her!

And then the wee lassie began to swim — 'Is this the way you do it, Mother, is this the way?' She began to swim out.

'Come back, dearie, come back,' she says, 'it's too deep oot there.'

And the wee lassie started to dive, to go up and under.

She says, 'Ye ken, ye're a good swimmer, wherever ye learned it, ye must hae been able to swim before.'

'No, Mother, it just cam tae me right away,' she said.

She says, 'Ye ken this, ye're a richt wee saltie!'

And that was the name the old woman gave her, from that day on she called her 'Saltie.' But Saltie stayed with them for another six months and she and the old woman were just the greatest of friends. Every day she used to go hawking with the old woman too, selling her baskets and tinware to the houses.

So one day she says, 'Mother, dae ye never get fed up on the sea? Dae yese never go on the roads?'

'Oh dearie,' she says, 'I hev sisters wanderin' the roads and I've never seen them for years, but my man likes the shore and he likes the sea, tae be on his own wi his twa sons on the sea. But my ambition is tae leave the sea, I'm fed up on the sea! I never see a soul, I never see nane o' my ain folk or nane o' my ain family. And I hev sisters and brothers on the mainland, traivellin folk, but I never see them fae day oot and day in.'

'Well, Mother,' she says, 'what would you really like to do, the best thing in yir life ye wad like tae dae?'

'Well, Saltie, what I would like tae dae, is tae pack up this sea-gaun life and,' she says, 'leave it, go back to the land and live on the land for a while because I'm fed up wi the sea — the salt in my blood!'

'Well,' she says, 'Mother, we'll hev tae try and do something aboot that for you, won't we!'

Now the two laddies were named Willie and Sandy. About two or three days later Willie picked up a bit rope he had tied at the back of the boat to go for a bundle of sticks for the fire.

When he picked up the rope Saltie said, 'Can I come wi ye and help ye?'

'Well,' he said, 'Saltie, if ye want to come, you can help me pack up some sticks.' This was the first time she'd ever been civil to Willie, the first time she'd ever asked to go with him. So they travelled about two or three hundred yards along the shore collecting driftwood and putting it in heaps along the shore. And she was clever at picking up the sticks, you know — her in her bare feet, never wore shoes!

'Willie,' she said, 'I hev something to tell ye.'

He said, 'What is it, Saltie?'

'Ye ken,' she said, 'your brother disna like you very much.'

He said, 'What?'

She said, 'Your brother disna like you very much.'

So he said, 'What makes you think that?'

'Well,' she said, 'last night while you were awa along the rocks fishin, I heard him talkin tae your father and he was tellin

him that you were lazy and he's tae dae all the work, he's tae
dae maist o' the rowin o' the boat and everything and all ye'll
dae is go and fish and gather sticks — he's tae dae the maist o'
the work!'

'Oh, is that the way o' it,' he says, 'is that the way they dae
it when I'm no aboot!'

'Aye,' she said, 'that's true, but dinna be tellin him I tellt ye!'

'All right,' says Willie, 'I'll no say a word about it.'

But the next night after they'd beached the boat and put the
tent up . . . Sandy's turn to go for sticks. She went with Sandy
and told him the same thing.

'Oh,' Sandy said, 'is that the way o' it?'

'I heard your father and Willie speakin aboot you last night,
Sandy. And,' she said, 'they were sayin' that you were lazy and
you didna dae half the work that they dae, and you'll no mak
nae baskets, you'll no help your father with the tin and you're
lazy — you just sit on the shoreside and wash your feet, ye'll
no help nae way!'

'Oh,' he said, 'is that what they're sayin!'

She said, 'They think they wad be better off withoot ye.'

He said, 'Is that what they think aboot me!'

'Well,' she said, 'dinna tell them I tellt ye!'

So that night they were gathered round the fire, the two
brothers started to argue and started to fight. The old father
tried to stop them and they fought each other.

So Willie, the oldest one (he'd be about eighteen), went to
the tent, packed up his belongings, and walked off. He said, 'If
yese can dae withoot me and I'm no good enough for to stay
with youse, I'll go on the mainland and find my uncles.'

So the next night after they beached the boat, the old man
went for sticks.

Saltie went with him. 'Ye ken, Sandy disna like you very
much,' she said, 'he blames you for his brother gaun awa . . . '
She told the old man all these stories.

The old man said, 'It wasnae my fault, he shouldna be fightin
his brother and he wouldna went away in the first place.'

'Well,' she said, 'he blames you! He was tellin me.'

'Was he tellin ye?' he said.

43

'He tellt me and Mother aboot you're the fault o' it,' she said, 'and he canna row a boat hissel.'

When the old man came back, he and Sandy had the biggest argument in the world. 'Well,' Sandy said, 'if that's the way you feel on't, I'll go on my way, and you can row the boat yoursel!'

The old man said, 'Ye canna leave me, I canna row a boat!'

'Well,' he said, 'if ye canna row a boat, ye can dae withoot a boat! I'm goin into the country to see my uncles. In fact, I'm fed up on the sea onyway, I'm sick o' the sea, I'm goin into the country. There's bound to be other places to live as wanderin a sea all the days of your life onyway.' He packed his wee bits o' belongings and he went away.

Now there's only Saltie and the man and woman left. So that night she said, 'Mother, I want to go for a swim.'

So they were sitting down at the shoreside before she went into the water. She said, 'Mother, are you worried?'

'Well,' she said, 'I'm a wee bit worried.'

She said, 'Are ye worried aboot Sandy and Willie? They're big young men, they'll manage to take care o' theirsel.'

'I think,' she said, 'they'll manage to take care o' theirsel, but what's about their poor father — he'll never in the world row that boat his ainsel because it's far too big for ae body.'

'Well,' she said, 'Mother, that's what ye wantit, isn't it! If he canna row a boat then he'll have to leave it, and if he leaves it, I'm sure you'll hev to go wi him!'

'Saltie, I never thocht that — maybe it's a good thing that Willie and Sandy went awa. If my auld man,' she said, 'leaves this boat and goes on the land, pro'bly I'll see my sisters and my brothers again, and the laddies if they ever meet up with them.'

'I'm sure,' she said, 'you'll see the laddies again.'

'I never thocht, Saltie, aboot that,' she said.

'Well, Mother,' she said, 'I'm gaun for a swim.'

So she took off her dress and dived into the water and she swam out, swam out and out, and the old woman waved her back, 'Come on, Saltie! It's too deep oot there, you might get yourself intae trouble.'

And just like that Saltie disappeared — she had held up her

hand and gien her a wave and then she was gone. The old woman waited and waited, she was greetin and roarin.

Up to the old man she went, 'That lassie has droont! She's disappeared, she's droont!'

The old man said, 'What happened tae her?'

She said, 'She went swimmin and she gied me a wave.'

'Look,' he said, 'that was nae lassie, woman. I knew all along, that was nae lassie. Woman, that was a silkie! That was your seal — cam back to repay ye for savin its life. But what I'm worryin aboot noo — hoo am I going to row a boat mysel?'

So the old man left the boat on the shore and rolled his bundle on his back and him and the old woman went on the mainland, never again did he go back to the sea. The old woman met her two laddies later on and all her brothers and sisters, and she told them the same story I'm telling you. But she never forgot Saltie the silkie.

THE CROFTER'S
MISTAKE

In Argyll in 1942 every little job you could get a shilling or a penny for meant the world to you. There was an old man retired from a stone quarry but who loved fishing. Old Duncan Bell and I were good friends. So one day he said to me, 'Duncan, would ye like to row the boat along tae Minard? We can dig a pail o' worms and I'll give ye a shilling.' I said, 'Sure, Duncan!'

So the old man got his small rowing boat and a graip, and we set along the shore; the old man sat in the back smoking Woodbine and I rowed, but when we pulled into the beach the tide wasn't full out. He said to me, 'Duncan, it'll be about an hour, maybe an hour and a half, before the tide is fit for hus to dig worms.'

Well, it was a nice day, and the bay below Minard was famed for seals. We sat on the beach and then a few seals came in. I said, 'Duncan, tae pass the time away, why don't you tell me a wee story?'

He said, 'Duncan, this story was told to me by my mother. As far as I believe, my granny and my great-granny came from the Outer Hebrides. This story could have happened oot in the Western Isles a long time ago, on Islay, Barra, Jura, Gigha, or any o' these islands.'

TALES OF THE SEAL PEOPLE

MANY MANY YEARS AGO in this island off the West Coast there lived two brothers. Now they had a small croft by the shoreside and naturally they were well off because their mother and father had died many years before and left them plenty of money. The youngest brother's name was Iain, the oldest brother's name was Angus. They had everything they needed — a small croft, a few cattle, and a few sheep and a few goats. But they also had a boat and did a lot of fishing in this island where they stayed.

Now Angus and Iain got on pretty well together after their parents had died. Iain used to go out fishing every morning and evening and he could bring in as much fish as he liked, it only took him a short while. But there was one thing Iain and Angus didn't have in common: Iain loved the seals and used to take fish out of his boat, fling them over the side to feed the seals if he thought he had enough. Now his brother Angus was upset about this.

'Iain, why is it that you feed these animals?' he said. 'I hate these things, these seals.'

And Iain said, 'Well, they hev tae live like you and I, Angus. Luik, we're well off, and we're only taking their food from them. A little bit that we dinna need would feed them.'

But Angus was a funny kind of brother, he was a bit morose. Sometimes he got angry and flared into some kind of temper, he was displeased about everything, nothing would content him. The thing he hated most in the world was seals, he hated them for evermore. And when Iain fed them a wee bit, gave them some fish, he said, 'Why didn't you bring it here? We could hev used the fish that you've thrown to the seals, and sellt the rest in the village.'

'But, Angus, brother,' he said, 'they have tae live!'

'Och,' Angus said, 'that's your way, but it's not mine.'

But it never came to a quarrel between the two of them. Iain would walk along the beach at night-time and spend all his time sitting on the rocks. The seals would come in around him and he wouldn't pay any attention to them, no way in the world — they were just his friends. But the minute Angus put his foot on the shore there was a splash, and the seals would be gone because he was bad. Anyway, life like that to the two brothers

48

was quite happy, they enjoyed each other's company though they didn't see eye to eye.

One day Iain took four boxes of fish to the market, along to the village where there was a pier. The people in the village were auctioning their fish, putting boxes up for sale. He met this beautiful lassie at the auction, she was standing all alone. She had a book in her hand and a pencil and was looking at all the fish and marking things down, but she wasn't buying anything.

So, after everybody had sold everything they had, and Iain had sold his four boxes of fish, the young woman was still standing there with her book in her hand writing things down. Everybody dispersed, walked away, but she still was standing. So Iain walked up to her. He was a handsome young man, tall, fair hair, blue eyes — the most beautiful man you ever saw.

'Hello!' he said. 'Eh, are you buyin or are you sellin?'

'Oh no,' she said, 'I'm not buyin, I'm not sellin, I'm just having a look to see how much fish is gettin passed, how much is gettin sold and how much fish is comin in.'

He said, 'Do you work for the government?'

'Oh, oh no, no, I don't work for the government,' she said, 'in no way.' Young Iain thought that she was a student working for the government or something, in these days taking stock of all the fish that was sold in the island. 'No,' she said, 'I'm just here to see what's going on, and see how much fish is passed through the sale.'

So after he had a nice talk to her, he invited her into a wee bar-room for a drink.

'Certainly! I'll go into the bar-room with you.' So they went into the fisherman's bar-room and they had a wee drink. It was an ale-house — this is many many years ago.

He asked her all the questions in the world about herself but she told him, 'I'm an orphan, I've no father and mother. I'm just on my own and I want tae make a record of how much fish is getting sold, how much fish passes through the sale in a year!'

'Oh,' Iain said, 'that's all right.' He didn't worry about it, you see! 'Why don't you come out home with me,' he said, 'tae the croft and we'll have supper together?'

So she went back with him, it wasn't far from the pier, about fifteen minutes' walk to where Iain stayed. When they landed back Angus was sitting at the table. Iain walked in.

Angus said, 'And hello, you're back, Iain, you're back.'

'Yes,' he said, 'I'm back. I sold the four boxes of fish and I got a good price for them, but I want you to meet this young woman I met at the saleroom. This young woman's name is Seda, her name is Seda and I met her at the market. She has no relations or no friends. She's callin a check on the fish.'

Angus was very morose, a very unpleasant kind of person, you know. Nobody liked him about the village, but everybody liked Iain. Angus was the kind of person you could never get to know. So he said, 'And what is the matter with wir fish, is there something wrong, are they not good enough or something?'

'No, no-no,' she said, after being introduced to Angus. 'No, Angus, that's not the problem at all. I'm just here to keep a check o' all the fish that the people catches and see how much they take out of the sea.'

'Well, we don't get enough!' he said. 'We could get more if it wasnae for those damn seals who keeps eatin our fish and destroyin our nets!'

And Iain said, 'Please, Angus, don't embarrass the woman — start talking about seals again — because ye know they need tae eat as well as us!'

'Och, that's the way you go about it — these *creatures*,' he said, 'who destroy wir livelihood!'

The young woman never said a word.

But after they had tea together Iain said, 'Can I walk ye back to the pier?'

'Oh no, I'm not gaun back to the pier,' she said, 'I want to go down to the rocks. They tell me that ye've a fine colony o' seals doon by yir croft here on the island.'

'Och, we hev hundreds o' seals,' he said.

And she said, 'Well, what do you think o' them?'

'Oh, they're just my darlings,' he said, 'I love them to my heart. There's nothing nicer in this world than watching the seals at play; and everything I can spare, though sometimes Angus is upset, I throw anything that I don't need overboard fir them tae have because they hev tae live too, you know.'

Angus said, 'There you go again, feedin these animals which are no good to anybody. Young woman,' he said, 'look, I'll tell ye the truth: I hate these things from the word go. They're destroying the things that's wir livelihood.'

So Seda said, 'Well, they're sea creatures.'

'Of course, I know,' he said, 'they're sea creatures, but why don't they swim along the shore and catch their own fish instead o' robbin wir nets and waitin till we catch fish for them!'

But Seda didn't argue in any way with him.

Iain said, 'Come on then, I'll walk ye to the rocks and show you the seals.'

'Look, I'll be all right,' she said, 'I'm sure you can find something else fir yoursel tae do.'

So Iain said, 'Okay,' and the young woman started to walk away. But he had a notion in his head that he loved this young woman. He called after her, 'Where can I see ye again?'

She said, 'You can find me if you want me!'

'Where will I find you?' he said.

'I'm only here for a short stay, but,' she said, 'part o' my time'll be spent watchin the seals on the rocks — if you want to find me, you'll find me there.'

So he bade her good-bye and she walked away to the rocks.

Angus turned around. 'Look, Iain, that's a queer creature! That's a queer kind of woman,' he said, 'I hope you're no thinkin that mebbe you and she can get together, because her opinions is not the same as mine. She's like you — she loves these creatures that destroys everything that we fought for, destroys wir nets and wir things.'

'But, Angus,' he said, 'the seals are people just like you and me, they need tae live, they need tae eat!'

'Well, they're not gaunnae eat out o' wir nets! They're catchin the things that we should catch!'

But Iain didn't want to argue with his brother Angus. So after everything was done Iain started out the door, to walk down to the beach to see his seals once more.

And Angus said, 'Where are ye gaun?'

'Ach, I'm going down to the beach,' he said, 'once more.'

'Och, you're going down there again, down again, among yir own kind of folk — you wouldnae stay and talk wi yir brother,' he said, 'and have a wee dram wi yir brother! Or find something else tae do. You would rather spend yir life doon with the seals — your kind o' folk!'

But Iain didn't want to argue with him. So he walked away down to the seal bay, and on the rocks, sure enough, there sitting was the young woman. She was enjoying herself and all the seals were playing themselves on the rocks — some were sitting basking in the sun, some were lying on their sides, and some were grunting and carrying on, doing all the things that seal people really do. And she really was enjoying it. So he walked down and sat beside her. They talked for a long long time. Iain fell in love with her, and he told her this.

'Look, Seda, I love you more than anything in the world. I'm a lonely man with my brother,' he said, 'and he's not an easy person tae live wi.'

'I have no people in this world,' she said, 'I'm only here for a short stay.'

So he invited her back to the house once more. Naturally, Iain fell more in love with Seda, and as time passed, to cut a long story short, they got married. And Iain brought her back to the house to live with him and his brother Angus. Angus didn't humour her very much, he didn't think very much of her, but Iain loved her from his heart. And they lived very happily. They did their own things: Iain went fishing every day, she helped out on the croft and did everything under the sun that needed to be done. She tried to please Angus to the best of her ability, but there was no way in the world she could. In the evening when they sat down by the fireside, all Angus's talk was about the seals, how much he hated them and how he hated the seal-folk. But Iain and his wife, they really loved each other, and when they got fed up and bored with Angus's talking, the two of them would move off to bed.

But one morning Angus was feeling not too well. Now they set nets for fish, forbyes taking care of the croft. And Iain said, 'I'll manage myself, Angus, seein you're not feelin too well.'

Seda carried up breakfast to Angus in bed, gave him a cup of tea. He wasn't very pleased, he never had a very good word for her. And she said to Iain, 'Angus is no able tae get up this morning.'

'Ach, I'll manage on my own,' Iain said.

So Seda kissed him farewell and wished him a good day. Iain took the boat and rowed away to set his nets and do his fishing.

Now Angus, he's lying upstairs in bed. So Seda busied herself around the kitchen, did everything that needed to be done — milked the goats and everything around the croft — the best she could do. She took Angus his dinner, up to him in bed, but he was still bad-tempered, spoke harshly to her. He couldn't even realize that his brother had a young wife and he had nothing! Possibly it was remorse that was bothering him more than anything else.

And every time she came up he was always saying, 'I hope he has a good day and I hope the seals disna bother him very much.'

But the day passed by and Seda came out — she waited at the doorway. She waited and waited. The day passed but Iain never came back. She went up and told Angus.

'Angus,' she said, 'Iain's not home yet.' Now it was about evening.

'Ach well, he's prob'ly out wi his friends,' he said, 'round the isle. Whatever you do, don't worry about him — he's prob'ly away feedin his friends in the island, his friends the seals!'

But the night passed by and Iain never came back; and the next day and the next evening, he never came back. And a week passed — he never returned. By this time Angus managed to get down on his feet, he was all right again. And Seda started to tell him about Iain disappearing in the sea.

She said, 'Angus, ye'll have to go and notify the police, tell the whole country that Iain is amissing, we've got to get his body back and bury him somewhere.'

'Och, he's gone,' Angus said, 'he's lost in the sea, prob'ly his boat capsized an he's drowned. You'll never see him anymore.'

There was a weeping and a wailing, and she cried, she was vexed. And she did everything; Angus never helped her very much. But Iain never returned. Angus bought another boat and she stayed on to keep house for him. Though the two of them couldn't see eye to eye, she did everything under the sun, but they could never exchange a sensible word between them.

Then one evening, she told him, 'Angus, I'm very sick.'

'What's wrong with you! Are you worried about your husband?' he said. 'He's gone with his *friends* — at's all ye need tae worry about — he's gone with his friends!'

'Angus,' she says, 'ye'll have tae go for the doctor.'

'Och, why am I to go for the doctor!' He says, 'Are ye ill or are ye sick or something?'

She says, 'Angus, I'm gaunna have a baby.'

'Och dear, oh dear-oh dear-oh me,' he says, 'you're gaun to have a baby — well, ye'll jist hev tae have a baby!'

It was an old bicycle he had, he cycled to the village and notified the doctor, the doctor came. Sure enough, Seda had a bonnie wee baby — a lassie!

Many weeks had passed since the disappearance of Iain and now there was a bonny wee baby, a girl had been born. And Angus began to change, he treated them very casually, very nicely.

He said, 'What are ye gaunna call her — the baby, the wee baby girl?' It was the first baby he'd ever seen in his life because he didn't have any sisters or brothers, but the one brother who was lost at sea.

'Well,' she said, 'Angus, I think I'll call her after myself, "Seda," after mysel.'

So they had reported to the authorities and they'd searched for Iain's body but he never was found, they found the boat but they never got him. 'Well, we'll have to make arrangements, you know,' he said, 'because this croft and the land is between my brother and me, and now if you want to stay here with your wee baby daughter, half o' this place, what my brother Iain owns,' he said, 'is yours. And I'm sure we'll try and get along together as best as possible.'

Seda was very pleased about this. 'There's nothing else I can do . . . where can I go? I've no place else to go,' she said, 'Iain was my husband and you are his brother.'

So they stayed in the croft and Angus went on doing the fishing. Seda took care of the croft and the animals, she milked the goats, took care of the cow, looked after the croft the best she could. And naturally wee Seda grew up to be the bonniest wee lassie in the world. When she started toddling round the croft, old Angus, the brother who'd be getting a wee bit old by this time, just loved her like nothing in this world — there was nothing he loved better than his wee niece! He cuddled her, kissed her and took her with him every place he went, took her sailing in the boat, taught her about the seals, told her how to hate the seals and how the seals had destroyed her father! But Seda didn't worry about this, she said, 'Okay, that's okay,' because she knew her uncle loved her.

But one night, after young Seda had grown up to be about six years old, she sat on the chair next to Uncle Angus. She loved him past the common.

Her mother, Seda, said, 'I want to take a walk. I'll see yese in a wee while.' She went for a walk down to the beach.

And Angus said to his niece, 'Come tae your Uncle Angus. Your mammy's gaun for a walk, and I'll tell ye a wee story!' So he told her a wee story, she fell asleep in his lap and he carried her up, put her to bed. He waited and he waited, he waited and waited, but her mother never came back. Her mother never came back from the beach. She just disappeared completely.

Next morning young Seda was crying for her mother. 'Your mammy's gone,' he said.

He walked down to the village, took Seda with him, reported her mother's disappearance to the police. They searched the shoreside, searched the village, everywhere, but Seda was gone, they couldn't find a trace of her! She was gone for ever. And Angus shook his fist at the shoreside. 'It's these people, these seal-folk, they've taken her away, they stole everything that I loved in this world! They take my fish, they took my brother and took my little girl's mother — I'll get revenge on these people in my own time in my own way.'

Now Seda was left with her Uncle Angus in this croft on her own. There was nothing else for him to do — she was six years old — he reared her up. Another six years passed and now she was twelve years old. She'd lived with her Uncle Angus all these days in this croft. And he'd sent her to school, walked to meet her and took her back, took care of her — he loved her like nothing else in this world!

But during this period Seda, when she had nothing else to do, would spend all her time on the beach sitting on the rocks, swimming out from the shore. The seals were her friends, she spent all her time with them. And Angus began to tell her about these people. 'Look, Seda, they took yir mother, they took your father, don't let them take you!'

She says, 'Uncle Angus, they never took my father.'

'Well, where's their bodies? Where have they gone? Your daddy's disappeared, yir daddy loved these people and yir mammy loved these people, and,' he says, 'you love them. Seda, luik, don't join these people! Because if ye do, ye'll be gone forever and they'll never return ye.'

'But,' she says, 'Uncle Angus, there's nothing to do with them — they're lovely. I love their life, they're free and they swim in the sea!'

He says, 'It's okay, they swim in the sea, and they come and steal my fish in my nets.'

'But,' she says, 'Uncle Angus, they hev tae live too, and they need something tae eat! They're jist like you and me, jist lovely creatures.'

Seda swam among the seals and she talked to them. The more she spent her time on the beach, the more Angus got upset. And he tried to tell her.

But one night he went on a drinking spree and he went home. When he landed there the house was dark. No tea was made, nothing. He searched for Seda, tottering about under the influence of drink. She was gone. He walked down to the beach, there she was sitting and about fifteen or sixteen seals were all gathered round her. He rushed down to the shore and caught her by the arm, he dragged her back to the house. 'Seda, I love you more than anything in this world, but,' he said, 'you'll never join these people.' So he took her into the house to where he used to kill the goats. He took a carving knife — 'Now, you'll never be able tae join these people. My father,' he said, 'and my grandmother told me a long time ago: there's only one way to stop a human fae joinin the seal people — when you chop off their fingers and you chop off their toes — I'm gaunna do the same tae you.'

'But, Uncle!' she screamed, and she shouted and she cried. But he held her fast under a drunken stupor and chopped off the points of her toes, and he chopped off the points of her fingers.

'Now,' he said, 'you'll never join these people and go away fae me!' Then he left her, with parts of her fingers and parts of her toes chopped off.

She never said a word, she never cried. She lay in her bed and suffered for two or three days. Angus came up and he coaxed her to have food, coaxed her to come down after he'd come to his senses. But no way would she speak to him — no way in this world, she wouldn't even talk to him! Seda lay in pain and agony for two weeks, never ate or never spoke for two weeks.

But finally it came a time when Angus had to go out on the sea to fish. As much as he loved Seda, he had his duty to perform and go for his fish. So this one day he took his boat and rowed out in the middle of the sea. And he said, 'At'll fix her. She'll never join them now because I love her too much. They took my brother, they took his wife, but they'll never take her!'

He rowed out in the boat in the middle of the sea and cast his net. The day was calm and beautiful, the sun was shining. 'Now,' he said, 'I'll have a good fishin today.' And he took the oars in his hands, he rowed the boat forward — but all in a moment he was surrounded by about a hundred seals. They came from all parts, they came round the bow of the boat and they came behind the boat and they came by the sides of the boat. They caused such a storm and such a disturbance around the boat, it capsized. The seals — dozens of them, old ones and young ones; big ones and wee ones — capsized the boat and he fell into the water. He tried to swim to the boat and up came the seals, they attacked him, snapped off the points of his fingers and they snapped off the points of his toes. He tried to get away but he was attacked from all angles, every single seal snapped at his fingers and snapped at his toes. They didn't want to do anything else. He swam as best he could, and when he reached the beach he looked at his hands — they were bleeding, his fingers were almost gone and his toes were almost gone. He sprauchled up onto the beach and lay for a long long time. His hands and feet bleeding, he crawled on his hands and knees, he was so exhausted when he reached his own croft — in a terrible state!

'Oh these cursed animals,' he said, 'they did this tae me, they took my fingers and they took my toes.' He looked at his bleeding feet, there was not a whole toe left. He looked at his hands, his fingers were nearly gone, snapped off by the seals! But he survived. They didn't want to kill him, just teach him a lesson. When he landed in the house he called, 'Seda, Seda, come and help me! Seda, please help me! I've lost my fingers, I've lost my toes — please, Seda, help me!'

But the house was empty. There was not a soul there, not a soul. He searched around, he walked, even though his feet were bleeding and his hands. He walked around the house, but Seda was gone.

So for two days he lay in agony and pain with his fingers and his toes. And he swore to himself. 'They did this to me, they'll never do it to me again. They took my brother, they took my sister-in-law, and they took my child that I really loved, even though I did such a terrible thing tae her when I was drunk. But,' he said, 'they'll never do this to me again.' And for four more days he lay in agony and pain with his fingers and his toes.

But after he came to himself and got himself fixed up, he said, 'I'm leavin, never more will I return to this place.' So with his hands bandaged and his feet fixed as best he could, he closed the door of the cottage. Taking all his belongings that he ever possessed, that he could carry, he says, 'I'm going.' And he shook his fist at the sea, 'I'll never return again! You can have it, Iain, you can have it, Seda; you can have everything I own, but,' he says, 'never again will you have the company of me!'

And he walked away, left the croft and everything behind him. He managed to walk to the village, got attention for his hands and feet, and he had enough money to keep himself for evermore. He said, 'I'm gaun off and find mysel a place in a glen far away from the sea, far away from the seals, where people disna know what a seal is.' And he went on his way . . . and he was gone.

About three weeks later, when the cottage on the shoreside was dark and the sun had set, three seals came swimming towards the croft. A big bull seal, a female seal, and a half-grown seal swam towards the beach. They looked at the cottage and the cottage was dark. One turned to the other and they nodded, they said, 'That is it!' But the funny thing was, the young, half-grown female seal, half her flippers were gone — half her tail flipper and her front flippers were cut across. They swam into the beach and looked at the dark cottage, the boat was pulled up and the nets were hung up to dry. The three of them came up on the beach and looked all around, then they turned and swam away. They were gone for ever.

The cottage remained waste, the croft remained empty for a very long time, till someone came along and bought it. But they never realized the story behind the croft, what had happened in that cottage. And that is the last of my wee story.

SEAL MAN

*The man who tellt me this silkie story was old Duncan Bell.
He was a cobble master, made stone bricks out of granite. He
was also captain of my shinty team. His family is still alive in
Furnace, he had a son and about eight daughters. We were
the dearest of friends. He liked me because I was called
Duncan like himself. I fished with him, rowed his boat and
dug his worms. Then he'd tell me stories about the seals. He
got this one from his granny, said his granny tellt him it. There
were a lot of good storytellers among the women, especially
among the crofting folk.*

ON A SMALL ISLAND on the West Coast a long, long time ago Jack lived with his mother. He had a good going croft, everything he needed in this world. Jack's father had died and left him well off. And his mother kept a few hens and ducks. That's all she did, take care of Jack all her life. Also along the shore on this little island where they lived were a lot of white houses, wee farm cottages. And mostly every person along the shore kept a boat because fishing was a big concern. When any fish were caught, they shared with each other what they could not sell.

Now his mother had an old friend, an old man called Duncan MacTavish. He would come visiting, sit cracking and smoking his pipe, talking about old times. He was a dear old friend, old Duncan MacTavish to Jack's mother. And Jack liked the old man very much. But Duncan was a fisherman. He'd fished all his life. He had known Jack since he was a baby. But the one love of Jack's life was the seals. Whenever Jack had the time to spare he'd walk along the beach collecting firewood, flinging out driftwood, collecting stuff. He was a kind of a beachcomber. But when the time came in the spring he would make himself a whistle from an ash tree. And Jack's enjoyment was sitting on the rocks playing his whistle to the seals. They would come round, gather round him. They would pop their heads up and sit up to the waves. Jack would play the whistle and Jack loved the seals to his heart. And he was always telling his mother about them.

His mother would say, 'There are many stories about seals, you see, Jack. They tell stories . . . that there's such a thing as seal men.'

'Aye, Mother!' he said. 'I don't believe in seal men. If there are seal men I've never seen any.'

'Laddie, look, there's seal men!' she said. 'I remember my granny a long time ago telling me when she was a lassie she'd seen a seal man walking along the beach, and he disappeared in the water.'

'Ach, Mother,' he said. 'That's only granny's cracks, old folk's tales!'

'Well,' she says, 'laddie, it may be old folk's tales, but it's true! There's such a thing as seal folk.' But Jack would not believe it, he'd never seen any. But anyway, he still loved the seals.

And old Duncan MacTavish used to always come along, maybe twice a week. And as Jack loved the seals old MacTavish hated them. He hated seals more than anything in the world. The only thing he never did was shoot them, because he was not allowed to keep a gun to shoot them with. If he'd had a gun he'd have shot every one. Because old MacTavish used to set a net and do a lot of fishing. When the seals came into his net, tore his net, he went raving mad. But if he got some fish, he would bring along a couple to Jack's mother for her and Jack's tea.

But one morning Jack was not too busy and the sun was shining. It was a beautiful morning. And he took a walk along the beach to collect more firewood or pick up his dry stuff he'd flung out the day before. And he came round, back beside a rock, no far from old MacTavish's house in the direction to the left of his own little cottage. There to his amazement lying at the back of a rock, with his head up on the shore, was a young man. And he was dressed in this kind of droll, kind of dark furry looking clothes. Bare feet. And dark, dark curly hair. He was face down in some seaweed. And Jack stepped forward. When Jack turned him over, half of the side of his face was all damaged. The blood — you could barely see his face! And Jack got an awful fright. He thought maybe the young man had fallen off a boat or something. He listened to the man's heart — he could hear it pumping strong. Jack said, 'He's still living!' And being a young, strong man, Jack got the young man on his arm, put him over his shoulder. He hadn't far to go. He carried him up to his mother's house. Into his own room, and he put the young man on the top of his bed.

Oh, and his mother cried, 'What happened? What happened, laddie, what happened?'

'Mother,' he said, 'it must have been an accident on the sea some place. Look, he's a young man. He's maybe been hit by a propeller of a boat or something. His head's in an awful mess.'

She says, 'Jack, wait a minute.' The old woman ran in and got the big metal kettle on the fire. And she got water in a wee enamel basin. With a bit of cloth she washed the side of his head. And he was lying there. His face was pale. Dark curly hair. She said, 'Jack, isn't he a handsome young man?'

'Aye,' said Jack, 'he is. But Mother, look, did you ever see the like of that?'

She says, 'What, laddie?'

He says, 'Mother, look at his fingers.'

And the old woman looked at the large snow-white hand. And his fingers were webbed like a duck's feet. In between his fingers were webbed. And Jack looked at his toes. It was the same thing. They were webbed too. 'Jack, brother dear,' she said, 'that's a seal man.'

'Nah, Mother,' he said, 'that's no a seal man. I heard my father tell me that you get folk born like that — with the skin between their fingers.'

'No, Jack,' she said, 'that's a seal man, laddie. God bless us, don't tell anybody!' So the old woman went and she bathed his face with water, and she had some kind of old spirits in the house or something. Then she patched it with goose grease and she put a bandage round his head, and she left him comfortable lying on the top of the bed. 'Come on then, Jack, let him rest a while. And I'll make you a cup of tea.'

But lo and behold they hadn't sat down long to make a cup of tea, when along came again old Duncan MacTavish. He had two-three fish on a string. And as usual he was in a raging mood. He came in.

The old woman said, 'Are you going to have a cup of tea, Duncan? We were just going to have a cup.'

'Tea,' he said, 'I'm not thinking about tea! If you could only see the mess of my nets, Mary. Have you seen the mess? You've no idea! With these blinking seals. God, that I was rid of them! They tore my nets. It will cost me a fortune to get them fixed. If I had a gun I'd shoot them all. But I'll tell you one thing, there's one of them will never bother me again. One of them will never trouble me.'

And the old woman said, 'What way? What happened?'

'Well,' he said, 'I'll tell you what happened. I got one of them today tangled in my net. And I got a right crack at him with a bell hook! He went down into the deep. And that was the end of him anyway. That's one of them anyway!' But Jack and his mother never said a word. But Duncan gave them the two-three fish. And he walked away.

'Mother,' he said, 'do you think — are you thinking what I'm thinking?'

She says, 'Jack, didn't I tell you — that's a seal man. And you'd better not tell anybody.'

'Oh,' he says, 'Mother, I'll tell nobody, not for the world.'

And she says, 'For God's sake, not a word to old MacTavish about this!'

So the mother and Jack sat and had their tea. They cracked a long long while. She says, 'Jack, do you think . . . we'll go and see that young man and see what like he is.' They went up to the room. The bed was empty. He was gone! Jack searched the house far and wide.

'But Mother,' he said, 'where could he go to? We could have hid him.'

She said, 'He must have slipped away while we were talking to old MacTavish.'

And Jack ran down to the beach. Nah! He wasn't there. He ran along the shoreside, round the house, searched the sheds. Nah, he was gone. The young man was gone. 'Well,' Jack said, 'at least we know he's not dead anyway.' And the young man was gone.

But two days later after the young man had went away, along came a commotion of a dozen folk from the village. They were searching the shores. Jack ran down and asked what was the trouble. They said that they found old Duncan MacTavish's boat. It had come in floating from the tide upside down. He was lost at sea. They found old Duncan's boat and they searched it. Then they searched the sea with boats for days and weeks. But old MacTavish's body never was found. He went a-missing.

Now Jack stayed with his mother for many many days, many many weeks. And the conversation was always about this young man. But Jack still continued playing his whistle to the seals. It never changed his life any, what had happened. But he always had one thought in his mind, if only he could have talked to him and spoke to him, asked him where he came from. Jack would have loved to. But anyhow, the weeks passed into months, and the months passed into a year. And it was summer time once again.

This was the time that Jack liked best. Because he could walk to where the sappy soukers grow along the shoreside. And he sat down one day with his knife and made another whistle with the bark off the sappy ash branch. After he got the whistle dried and cleaned, took all the sap off and put the bark back on, he would begin to play a wee tune. And he would go down to the rocks and sit there, play his whistle on the rocks. But he always had the thought in his memory, I wonder what happened to the wee seal man that he carried up from the beach. When he looked — up came half a dozen seals right out in front of him, not very far away!

And this one came up a bit closer. They came in close to Jack, not more than about five or six feet away. They stood there and watched him. And one came up to Jack's waist, and put his head from side to side. Jack could see a grey white patch round the side of its head. The hair had turned white, snow white on the side of his head. And it watched Jack for a long long while. Then Jack stopped the whistle — and like that, the seals were gone. Jack felt awful sad at heart.

He said to himself, 'I'll never see him again. I'll never even speak to him! But at least I know he's still living.' And he went back and tellt his mother the story I'm telling you. He said, 'Mother, you wouldn't believe what happened!'

She says, 'What? You never saw him again?'

'Aye, Mother!' he said. 'I saw him again.'

She says, 'Do you believe me now, Jack, he was a seal man?'

'Aye, Mother,' he said, 'it was a seal man.' And Jack lived with his old mother there till his old mother died. He lived in that croft all his life, but he never again had a chance to see the seal man. And that's a true story.

BLIND ANGUS

I came across this story by having a visit to a little hotel away in the North of Scotland in the 1940s. Now this story is very old, perhaps the oldest silkie tale I know. There's no point in me telling you where the story actually came from because we don't really know. Many people have different versions of the same story. I could say one place, and people lay claim to it in another. But the story as I know it began in the Western Isles a long time ago.

IT WAS ALL BECAUSE OF a cattle dealer called Angus MacLean. Now Angus bought cattle from the local farmers and he kept them for a while, because he had a small croft. He didn't keep any cattle of his own. But he fattened those he bought in, and then sold them to people who wanted to buy them. Now he would take a few cattle to the market, and there he would sell them. He bought all the lean cattle he could find. He was known as Angus MacLean the Cattle Dealer!

To some people Angus was a bit of a rogue because he tried to cheat — well, he was a dealer! Cattle dealers try their best to survive in their own right. Some people loved him, some respected him. Some said he was a rogue, some said he was a hero. But Angus was not only a cattle dealer. When people used to kill cattle for their own domestic purposes in the Western Isles, Angus would buy the skins of the cattle. Because people who needed a bit of meat to survive would kill an animal on their own. It was legal to do that on the Western Isles, to kill a beast if you'd reared it up. Like a shepherd killing a sheep. And of course Angus would buy the skin, take it home, stretch and dry it. But not only the skins of domestic animals did Angus buy; he also bought the skins of seals. Now people who had no cattle of their own made a living from killing seals, salting the skins and selling them. Sealskins were used for many purposes. Bagpipe makers would buy sealskins for making their bags. And of course Angus was famed for buying sealskins!

Angus went to the local cattle market one morning and he had a fine cattle beast that he had bought from somebody. He had kept it for a few weeks, maybe ten or twelve. But he had fattened it up. He took it to the market, and knew he would sell it for a good price because it was fat. Maybe a local butcher would buy it. But as he walked into the market of the small village, the first person he met was a tall dark man dressed in black, wearing a long dark cloak.

He walked up to Angus and said, 'That's a fine beast you have there.'

Angus said, 'Well, it's for sale, you know, and I am a cattle dealer. I don't only deal in cattle. I also deal in hides. If you want any hides, if you have any use for hides, skins or anything; I deal in sheep skins, in cattle skins and sealskins!'

'Oh I see,' said the tall dark man dressed in a long, dark cloak. 'You also deal in sealskins, do you?'

He said, 'Yes.'

'And have you many at home?'

'Well,' Angus said, 'well, there's a certain fellow who kills a few seals and he gives me the skins. I salt them and I stretch them, and sell to the local people who need them. Would you be interested in the sealskins?'

The man said, 'No, not really. I'm more interested in this cattle beast you have.'

And Angus said, 'Well, would you like to buy her?'

And the tall dark man said, 'Of course, I would like to buy her! But you see I have a problem.'

Angus said, 'Well, what's your problem?'

He said, 'I would like to buy your cattle beast. But you see, I would like you to take her out to the island, the little island out there.'

'That little island?' says Angus. Now beside the village where the people were selling in the market there was a little island in the bay, about a mile out. But it was uninhabited. Nobody was on the island. And Angus thought this strange. He said, 'You mean Lear Isle?'

He said, 'Would you like to go out?'

Angus thought this was very interesting. He said, 'Yes.'

The man asked, 'What is your name?'

'My name is Angus MacLean.'

'Well,' he said, 'Angus, I'll pay you well for that cattle beast because it's nice. If you would take it out to Lear Isle for me.'

But Angus said, 'What do you do out on Lear Isle? There's nothing out there. No habitation of any kind. There's not even a building or a tree.'

He says, 'That's my problem. But I'll tell you, Angus, if you're willing to sell your beast to me, and if you could hire yourself a boat and row that beast out . . . ' Now the custom was on the Western Isles, if you had to take a beast to an island, you put a rope on it and you put it behind the little rowing boat. You rowed and the beast swam behind the boat. That's the way they transported cattle a long time ago. He said, 'I'll pay you in guineas. Gold guineas. What would you be wanting for your beast?'

'Well,' he said, 'I would like about ten guineas for her.'

'Ten guineas?' said the tall dark man. 'That's reasonable. But I'll tell you what I'll do with you. I'll give you twenty gold guineas if you will take her out to the Lear Isle for me and put her on the island.'

But Angus said, 'There's nothing out there! There's not even grain for a beast.'

And the man said, 'That's my problem! Could you hire yourself a rowing boat? And you and I will row the beast out to the island. Deliver it there and I will pay you twenty gold guineas for your beast!'

'Done, sir!' he said. So Angus had an old friend he knew he could borrow a boat from. Now he never got the length of the market. He led it down the causeway to the beach. And he talked to an old friend of his who had a rowing boat. He explained the purpose. And he said, 'Old man, I'll give you a guinea for a loan of your boat to take her to the wee island.'

And the old man who knew Angus well said, 'That is fine, Angus, there's no problem. You can borrow the boat. I'm not using it.'

So Angus and the tall dark man went in the boat. They took the cattle beast behind on the rope. Now Angus said, 'You'll have to row the boat.'

'Oh,' the tall dark stranger said, 'I'll row the boat, no bother. It's no problem to me, if you'll keep the animal behind the boat. And as I row just make it swim to the island.' It wasn't far out. 'But,' he says, 'there's something I must do before we go out. Angus, I must blindfold you.'

Angus said, 'Blindfold me, what do you want to blindfold me for?'

He said, 'Look, it's no problem, Angus, I won't hurt you. All I want you to do . . . ' And he took from his pocket a black handkerchief. He said, 'Angus, all I want you to do is tie this across your eyes.'

'What do you want that across my eyes for?' he said. 'I'm leading the beast. You'll be rowing.'

'Angus, when we land on the island,' he says, 'I don't want you to see what's there.'

Angus said, 'There's nothing to see! Why do you want me to put a handkerchief across my eyes?'

He said, 'Angus, I'm telling you, I want you to put this across your eyes! It'll no hurt you. And I'll pay you well. In fact, I'll give you another extra five gold guineas if you put the handkerchief around your eyes!'

'Well,' Angus said, 'there's no problem.'

He said, 'You don't need to help me beach the boat. We'll take care of it.'

'*We'll* take care of it?' Angus said.

'Oh,' he said, 'we'll take care of it.'

But Angus said, 'It's only you . . . and I don't see why you're going to take this animal to an island to live on its own! There's nothing out there but rocks and stones.'

The tall stranger said, 'Angus, it's my problem, not yours! I'm paying you well.'

'Well,' Angus said, 'if that's the way you want it, that's the way it will be!'

So Angus got in the back of the boat, the big cow on the rope. And the stranger got in the front. But before he went in the front of the oars, he took the black handkerchief and tied it around Angus' eyes. And tied it behind his neck. He took the oars and he began to row, Angus with the rope behind the boat with the cattle beast. He rowed out to the island. And of course the cow, once it got into the water it began to swim. Cows can swim very well. And he rowed the boat very gently out to the little Lear Isle. The cow went plod, plod, plod behind the boat. And the man beached the boat. The tide was out and there was a little strand. Then the stranger got out of the boat and he walked around, took the rope from Angus' hand.

He said, 'Thank you, Angus,' and he led the beast up the beach. But the moment the animal was away, Angus put his hands up and he took the handkerchief from his eyes. And he looked. Angus stared in amazement. For the island was full of people! There were dozens; old men, young and old people. They rushed forward to the beast. An old man with a grey beard rushed forward. And within minutes they took the beast

71

and cowped it on its back. A dozen of them, they cut its throat. And in minutes they killed it and they butchered it on the island. Angus was amazed! He pulled up the hankie, back over his eyes because he couldn't . . . he never saw a beast butchered so quickly in all his life. He stood there with the handkerchief over his eyes. Where did all these people come from? Angus hadn't a clue. Within minutes they had killed, butchered, quartered an animal in front of his eyes on an island where there was no one! In minutes the tall black man, dark stranger came back once again.

He said, 'It's all right, Angus. It's fine now. Let's row back to the mainland.' And he turned the boat and rowed back again. Angus pulled the handkerchief down. They beached the boat on the mainland. And the man took a purse from his pocket, and he counted out twenty-five gold guineas. 'There you are, Angus,' he said, 'and thank you.' He walked away.

Angus stood there. Now he had the money in his hand. More money than he'd ever had for a long time. Twenty-five guineas. He said, 'What in the world had happened? What was going on out there on that island?' But then he went back home to his wife. He never said a word to her. But deep in his mind he was still thinking about these things that happened on the island. He swore he saw people butcher that animal on that island. But nobody was there!

But anyway, a week was to pass. Angus bought another lean old animal. He had many. He fattened him up in his little croft. Two weeks later it was market time again. Angus picked the fattest beast he could find among his animals. He'd sell another one in the market. And he walked down to the local village once again with another beast. As he walked into the village there were many farmers around and villagers around, people doing their local business. As he walked the beast up, up comes the man once again! The same man Angus had met before.

'Hello, Angus,' he said.

'Oh hello,' said Angus, 'hello!'

He said, 'That's another fine beast you have.'

'Aye,' Angus said, 'she's not bad. She's put the weight on. She's fat and full. I think I'll sell her well.'

He said, 'Angus, would you sell her to me?'

Angus says, 'No! No way I'm going to sell another beast to you.'

'And why, Angus,' he said, 'are you not going to sell another beast to me? What's the problem? Didn't I pay you well for the last one?'

Angus said, 'You paid me well. And you made me row out to the island. And you butchered that beast in front of my eyes! I never saw an animal killed so fast in all . . . '

'Oh,' he said, 'Angus, so you did — didn't you see?'

Angus said, 'I did see. I saw things I never saw in all my life! That island was bare. There was no one there. And I saw people there. And I saw an animal butchered in front of my eyes like I've never seen an animal butchered before in all my life.'

'Oh I see,' said the stranger. 'Well, Angus,' he said, 'you will never see anything again as long as you live!' And he took his fingers like that — snapped his fingers in front of Angus' eyes. And Angus felt something like sand or dust going into his eyes. And he closed his eyes. It hurt for a few moments. And Angus looked, but Angus could not see. Angus was blind.

Of course the stranger walked away. But for Angus, he never saw again. He became known as Blind Angus the Cattle Dealer. But Angus told that story to many people. No one ever believed him. So you've heard the story from me. And probably you won't believe it. But that is a true story, what happened to Angus the Cattle Dealer a long time ago.

THE LIGHTHOUSE
KEEPER

Away back in the West Coast a long time ago, there once lived a lighthouse keeper. He lived on the mainland and he had a wife and two children. But every four months he used to go out to this lighthouse on a rock off the coast. And the keeper was in that lighthouse on the rock for three months at a time. It was a hard time to be a lighthouse keeper in these days because the pay was poor and you were cut off from everybody; you never saw your relations, you were very lucky if a boat ever came to you. Now this old keeper's name was Peter MacKinnon. He came back to the mainland for a month after his time was served on the rock; he called it 'The Rock.'

One night I was lucky to meet Peter in a pub. He was a wee bit upset as he sat in the bar-room of this wee pub. And I could see by the way he told this story to us — we were sitting round the table listening — that he really believed it. I don't know if you'll believe the story or not, I don't know what you'll feel about it, but this is the way Peter told it to me.

THE BOAT PUT ME OUT on the island, on The Rock, with a wee bit provisions, and the things which were to keep me for three months at the lighthouse. I took these off the boat and they said, 'Well, if the weather's good, we'll prob'ly see ye in a couple o' months.'

So I gathered all the wee things and put them in the room, I put them all by where I would need them. And I'd been there for a couple of weeks, the weather was kind of rough — really rough. On The Rock there was a path leading down to the shoreside, it was the only way you could get down to the water, the one path on The Rock. But for days and days I sat in the lighthouse, nothing to do but light the lamps and read the papers, no letters or anything coming from anybody. I would be lucky if there would be another boat for a couple of months.

But one day the weather changed. The sun came out and the sea was calm. I was kind of bored sitting and I said, 'Ach, I'll take my rod and walk down the path, because the sea's no so rough today. I'll walk down the wee path. I'll maybe catch mysel a couple o' fish and pass away the time.' So I took my rod and walked down. The night before was a terrible storm but this morning was calm. I would try and catch a few fish for my tea. But I never got my fly wet.

I was just about to cast it, a yellow seafly to fish sea trout with, when lo and behold I looked beside The Rock and there against the wall among a puckle seaweed was a seal! And it was lying on its side, the waves were hitting it against The Rock. I could see by the look on it that it wasn't dead.

I had my wellingtons on, which I usually use when I go fishing, for the spray that washes off the rocks. So I walked down, I caught her and I lifted her up. I could see she was still alive. I said to myself, 'You've been sick or you've mebbe been caught in a heavy tide last night and you might be ill. Ye've had a bad time o't, little creature. I better take ye up and see if I can do something for ye.'

So instead of fishing that day, I laid my rod against the wall, I said, 'I'll get you later on.' I took the seal and it was still alive, I could see that it had a good bit of life in it! So I carried it up and it wasn't very light, it was nearly a half-grown seal and a female. I carried her up in my oxters. I was glad to see something for company because I hadn't a kitten or a pup or even a mouse in the lighthouse. I carried her right up, I soothed her the best I could.

I put her on the bed, she was very sick, ill, as I thought she was. But I looked around her and saw there was no damage attached to her, there wasn't a hurt, no bleeding or anything. 'Ach,' I said to myself, 'she's prob'ly exhausted.' She was about six or seven months old. I put her in the bed and happed her up with a blanket. I said, 'Keep yoursel warm there.' So I went into the kitchen, I made a drink of condensed milk and fed her with it.

She drank the milk and I said to her, 'Little creature, you be quiet there, be kind and stay yirsel, stay there in bed and ye'll be all right because Peter'll take care of ye!' But now by the time I had got her up to the room and given her a drink, evening began to come — evening came very early. I had to go up the stairs to light the lamps. So I left her there in bed by herself after her drink and she was quite contented.

I lighted the lamps, cleaned the reflectors, got the lights set for the evening, and I came down. But by the time I came back down she seemed to have recovered a wee bit. Then I went and made a wee bit of supper for myself. I had my supper and came back in, I said, 'Are you all right, are you feeling fine now?'

But, och me, God, she was up in bed, she was sitting up fine as could be! Maybe she was a wee bit exhausted. But lo and behold, I had some dried fish and I gave her some, she just gobbled it up as quick as could be. And after she gobbled the fish she seemed to rally as best as could be and I said to myself, 'You're not damaged in any way, you're not hurt and not sick . . . you're a good friend and I hope you'll stay with me a long long while.' And we began to be good friends.

But lo and behold, I had sat down just for a minute, when she flapped upon the floor. And she flipped and she flapped around the whole place as if nothing had been the matter. I said to myself, 'That's kind o' queer.' But to me it was exciting just to hear her flippers flapping along the floor. And she went through the whole kitchen, through the whole place, and this 'flip-flap' . . . you know, it's very hard when you live in a light-house on your own out in the sea and there's not a soul to be

77

seen or not a voice or anybody to speak to or anything, and you're on your own. Even a mouse would cheer you up! When somebody comes flip-flapping around the floor, especially a seal that you have just taken from the sea, it means so much to you — it means the world to you. So I said to myself, 'If you're gaunnae flip-flap around the floor as much as that and keep me happy, I'm gaunnae call you "Flippy."'

Anyway, I called her Flippy and she flipped around the floor, she was so happy. I fed her the best food I could find. She and I became the best of friends. So after a couple of weeks I said to myself, 'That is not just a natural seal. She's so free and so easy that it seems tae me she's been someone's pet or something, that someone had her before. And she's so intelligent.' She was just like a puppy to me.

My wife had packed my bag for me that last time I left. She'd said, 'Peter, when you're walking round the lighthouse, always remember your slippers.' So when she'd packed, she'd put my slippers in the bag — instead of putting two slippers in, she put three in the bag. So I had them on my feet, but there's always one left I didn't have a neighbour for. Now in the evenings when the lamps were lighted and after I had my supper, Flippy and I would sit there in the room. I used to throw the one slipper to her. And just like a good dog she would bring it back to me, and I would throw it again. Oh, and this was fantastic, it would pass away the time.

Days passed by. Then one evening I was tired and I lay on the bunk bed. Flippy wasn't very pleased playing with one slipper, but she had to take my other two. So I thought to myself, 'Mebbe I could teach her a wee trick or two.' So I threw one slipper and she brought it back and left it down, then I threw another and she brought it back and left it down, then I threw another slipper to her, she brought it back and left it down — would you believe it, she left them all in a row! Now this began a game with me and her. Every time I threw a slipper she brought it back. I threw one and another and another, and she'd always bring them back, leave them in a row.

Flippy and I spent three or four weeks together. But I could see that she was longing for something. I said to myself, 'Flippy, I know what you're longin for,' because sometimes I felt that

78

she felt very sad. One day I said, 'I think it's about time I took ye back to the sea tae get back among yir own people.' By this time she had grown bigger and I was sad to see her go, sad to part with her. But I carried her down the steps. And there beside the wall was my fishing rod, lying where I'd left it three weeks before.

It took me just bare than busy to carry her down the steps and put her in the water. She swam away, went round two or three times and dived two or three times. She swam out, and I thought she would come back. But I wasn't worried so much because I didn't want to make a pet of her, I knew it would just be ruining her life. She swam for a while, I sat and I cast awhile with my fishing rod. But I never had a bite. I watched Flippy, she circled two or three times, stood up in the water, and then she was gone. And believe me or not, as I'm telling you this story I swear on my mother's grave, she was gone for evermore. I never saw her again.

Now I was kind of sad, but delighted that she was healthy enough to go. I had made her well, and she could go on her own way, because seals need their own people. I took my fishing rod, but I never had any luck that day, so I walked up, and put my rod by in the cupboard. Then the wind began to get up. The storm blew. It blew and I lighted the lamps. I kept inside for a couple of days. And the storm blew harder. For two days I never saw outside the window. But I knew that in another two or three weeks or a month I would be relieved, I would be back with my wife and family. I could tell them the fantastic tale about the seal and how I enjoyed her company. But that would be a long time yet.

Then, about a week later, a terrible thing happened. As you know, I had to walk up the stairs, which are circular, to the lamps. I walked up the steps, I was lighting the lamps, and I opened the window. A gust of wind came straight in after I lighted the lamps, hit me straight in the face. I never knew that the gust was so strong. I stepped back, I slipped, fell, fell down the stairs — three turns down. I couldn't help myself. I hurt my shoulder, hurt my arm, I hurt my head and I'm lying there. I knew that I had made a terrible mistake. I lay there semiconscious and I knew my arm was broken because I had no feelings in it. I had a terrible bash on my head. I thought to myself, 'What's gaun to come of me, because it'll be a week or a fortnight, maybe three weeks' — you lost track of time when you're on your own in one of these lighthouses. I said to myself, 'I am not gaunnae survive with this arm, how in the world — when it's broken!'

So I lay in the doldrums, and I would have given the world if I could have crawled to the room, got myself a wee drink or something. But I'm lying there in a semi-conscious state when I heard the flip-flip-flip, flip-flip-flip-flip coming ben towards me. I said to myself, 'It's only one person in the world could make that sound, it must be Flippy has come back!' I lay there, oh, I was in pain and misery. And I heard in my mind the flip-flip-flip of the feet on the causeway coming into the room where I lay. I only had one thought in my mind, it was Flippy the seal, she'd probably missed me and come back. She'd be company to me even though I was in agony.

Then lo and behold, I looked up, and standing beside me — as sure as I'm here — was a young woman, the most beautiful young woman I had ever seen in my life. She was standing there as if she was standing here beside me now, this young beautiful creature with long dark hair and a tight-fitting dress on her that you never saw before in your life! Through the mist of pain and darkness — the light was only shining faintly from above — I turned round and looked up, I thought I was in a dream. I said, 'My dear, where did you come from?'

And she looked down and said to me, 'Are you hurt?'

I said, 'Yes, I'm hurt. I fell from the landing, from the lights. I tumbled down the stairs and landed here. I've hurt my head and I think my arm is broken.'

She bent down and said, 'Come and I'll help you.'

So she helped me up, and you may believe it or not, she oxtered me in and put me on my bed. There by the light I had a good look at her. I saw that she was the most beautiful creature that I ever saw in my life, with long dark hair and dark eyes, and this tight-fitting kind of dress on her and her bare feet. She said, 'I'll help you!'

But I said, 'In the name of creation, dearie, where in the world have you come from?'

She said, 'Never mind about me, I'll tell ye about me later. We'll think about you first because you are sick and ill and hurt, and I am not. We'll get you fixed up first.'

So believe it or not, she put me in bed, she took off my boots. She took my arm, got it set, she spliced it — a doctor or a specialist couldn't have done a better job. And she bathed my head with water, made me feel comfortable. I lay there in a semi-conscious state believing I was in a dream. But there she was standing before me . . . I finally fell asleep.

I wakened to the flip-flap, flap-flap-flap in the morning. And would you believe me what I'm telling you, you probably won't, but it was the flip-flap of her bare feet on the floor that sounded so much like the flippers of my seal who had gone weeks before.

She sat down on the bed beside me and said to me, 'Drink this. This is something that'll make you well.' She had a cup in her hand, one of my mugs.

I said, 'What is it?'

'Oh,' she said, 'never mind what it is. Just you drink it, it'll make you feel better.'

I was so amazed, I didn't understand — I just drank this to please the young woman, not to insult her. To see a young creature in a lighthouse miles away from the land . . . I was in such a state, I didn't know was I coming or going. But I took the cup from her hand and I drank, the first taste was like seaweed. I've had pieces of seaweed, because in my old father's time along the shores years and years ago, Father used to say that sucking a piece of dry seaweed was good for you. It was full of iron. This stuff in the cup tasted the same, and sure and behold I hadn't drunk it for very long when I felt better, a lot better.

Well, to make a long story short, she tended me all that day and all that night. By the next morning I felt even better and the dizziness in my head was gone. My arm felt a wee bit better. So I sat up in bed and said to her, 'Young woman, where in the world have you come from? To come to this lighthouse well away from the mainland is just something that's unexplainable.'

'Well,' she said, 'tae tell ye the truth, I wis out in a fishin party with a few friends and the storm came up. The boat capsized. Everybody swam fir their life and I got lost in the storm, I saw yir light and I swam here. I saw yir lighthouse and I knew I'd find refuge, but I don't know what happened tae the rest of my friends.'

I said, 'Tae tell you the truth, there's no communication between here and the mainland. The next boat . . . will be weeks before it arrives and there's nothing we can do about it. I'm sorry for your friends, but you're lucky that you managed tae survive.'

She said, 'I hope they'll survive the same way as me. But in the meantime, if we're gaunnae be here till the next boat comes, we'd better get tae know each other.'

'Well,' I said, 'my name is Peter MacKinnon.'

She said, 'My friends call me Rona.'

'If me and you have tae be here together,' I says, 'fir the next couple o' weeks — let me see now, it'll be a fortnight anyway before the boat comes again tae relieve me from the lighthouse.'

She said, 'By that time you should be fit and able tae be on your feet.'

But sure enough, the next day I felt ten times better! Och, I felt better than ever I felt in my life, but for this damned arm that was broken! But she'd set it and put a sling around my neck. And I got around the lighthouse, I was doing everything I could with one hand.

So we sat evenings out and we talked of many things, but she would never talk about her people. A week had passed. She cooked for me and tidied up, she did everything for me that I really needed done. And I loved her like nothing on this earth. She was just like the wee lassies back on the mainland.

After ten days had passed I began to get a feeling in my fingers, they began to feel better which shouldn't have been for weeks! But she still kept giving me these cups of evil-tasting medicine, like seaweed. After a few more days I began to rally and come to myself again. I promised to take her back to the mainland in the ship and introduce her to my wife and my sons. I loved her like my own daughter because I didn't have any daughters, I just had two sons. So I sat and told her cracks and tales and stories, I told her about Flippy the seal and how Flippy and I had spent such times together, how vexed I was when Flippy went and left me, how lonely it is for an old man like me to spend three months on a rock out in the sea with nobody to speak to for days on end. And we became great friends. She did everything, I had nothing to do. I felt perfect except for this damned arm, but it got better every day.

Then one morning the sun shone brightly and clearly. I was lying in my bed. Rona used to always come in and give me a cup of tea every morning and waken me up because she slept in another wee room in a cubby hole in the cupboard where I made a bed for her. But I waited and waited, waited and waited for my morning cuppy, which I had got accustomed to. It never came. I managed to get up on my own, and this time my arm felt a bit better. And I knew that within a week the boat would relieve me, I would be back home to my wife. I could see my own doctor, get it fixed perfectly. I waited and I called around the lighthouse, around the rooms. There was not a sight of her to be seen. I searched every place I could find but Rona was gone.

I went back to my bedroom and I sat, I worried. I had no time for tea, nothing. I was so vexed and so sad I didn't know what to do. I had no time for breakfast, I was so sad. I said, 'Prob'ly she went out swimmin and she got drowned.' And I was so upset, I didn't know what to do. I searched the island, I went down the steps, searched the lighthouse outside and inside. She was gone, there was no Rona.

I came back up the steps and said, 'I wonder where in the world that wee lassie has gone.' And I walked into my bedroom, to the bed right there where I slept. And what do you think was staring me right in the face? Now you're not going to believe this, but the room was empty, the lighthouse was empty, and Rona was gone. But there were three slippers left in a row in front of my bed. Three slippers — left in a row in front of my bed! I knew then that Flippy had come back to help me for helping her, for she was a silkie! And that's the end of my story.

SEAL BROTHER

When I was thirteen I ran away from home to make room for the other children coming up. I was seventh of sixteen in our family. If there was any food around, it was for them — you couldn't take a crust from your wee brothers' mouths. So I spent some time in Kilberry between Ardrishaig and Tarbert with an old rabbit catcher called Angus MacNeil. I used to walk with him, carry his snares on my back and his rabbits from the hill. He killed and trapped rabbits for a living. And one evening by the fire-side I said, 'Angus, do you have any stories, any about the seal people?' 'Well Duncan, I'll tell you a true story,' he said, 'that happened a long time ago. Now it's a very old story and it was told to me in Gaelic by my grandmother.'

TALES OF THE SEAL PEOPLE

IF YOU WERE TO TRAVEL to the West Coast of Scotland there beside a little village is a graveyard. And in there is a little tombstone shaped like a heart. On that tombstone are four words that say, 'To Malcolm and Mary'. People have often wondered why it doesn't say anything else, no dates of birth or anything, just the four words. In bygone days the path leading to the graveyard was just earthen, and during the cold and rainy days when people visited the graveyard the path got very wet. Sometimes it turned to mud. If you were to visit that little graveyard today you would find the path leading to that heart-shaped stone is gravel. But in bygone days it was just a muddy little road.

My story takes you back more than a hundred years to a crofting family who lived by the shoreside not far from the village. The man's name was Donald MacDougall and his wife's name was Margaret. Now Donald and Margaret were very happy. They kept a few animals. But Donald's main thing was fishing, where he spent most of his time while Margaret took care of the little stock they had, maybe a few goats or a few sheep, and hens and ducks of course. But it was the happiest family anyone could ever think of. The reason was they had two children, twins. The boy's name was Malcolm and the girl's name was Mary. They were born on the very first day of March, a month beginning with 'M'. This was how Malcolm and Mary got their names.

And of course the children attended the local village school. But these children being twins were devoted to each other. Not like children you have today, as Angus would tell you. These children really loved each other, more than anything else in the world. And Mary helped her mother and Malcolm helped his father. There was nothing these children would not do for their parents. And the parents loved them dearly. During the meal-times if there was a little extra food left over Mary would say, 'Oh, give it to Malcolm!' Malcolm would say, 'No, give it to Mary!' But they never argued, they never fought. Then at the weekends they spent most of their time on the little island not far from where they lived in the little croft.

They would ramble along the beach, play all day long and their parents knew they were quite safe. They were free from

86

all the wide world and were so happy. At night-time they
wandered home, their cheeks rosy with the fresh air. Of course
they'd have their meal and sit down there. And father would
tell them stories and Mary would tidy up the kitchen, help her
mother. But when Malcolm and Mary were on the island, they
were completely devoted to each other. Sitting on the beach
together Malcolm would hang his legs over the rock. He was a
powerful swimmer from the age of five. Malcolm could swim
like a fish! But there was one thing that annoyed Mary — it
didn't really annoy her, but she used to torment Malcolm about
it. Malcolm was born with an enlarged toe on his right foot.
And she would make fun of the toe. Of course he didn't take
it too seriously.

But when he hung his legs over the rock before he went off
swimming she would say, 'Malcolm, that's a terrible looking toe
you've got.'

'Well,' he says, 'Mary, I can't help it. My parents gave it to
me, I'll just have to live with it!'

She tormented him, but she loved her brother dearly. Now
Malcolm's obsession was swimming. And of course on that
island where they played were many many seals. And many's a
long evening these children would sit there among the seals. The
seals were so used to the children they didn't pay much attention
to them. Malcolm would dive in among the seals and he would
swim.

Mary would say, 'Malcolm, if you don't stop it you'll turn
into a seal!'

He would come out and sit on the rock and say, 'Mary, that's
the only ambition I have. I love these creatures! I wish I could
be one of them. Look how they can swim, look how they can
dive! Where do they go to?' These children loved the seals, and
of course the seals paid them no attention.

The children grew up and they went to the same little school
in the village. But time passed by and both of them left school
at the same age of fourteen. And when they finished they came
back to work with their parents. Malcolm went to sea with his
daddy. He was good with a boat and could do anything. The
parents had very little to do because now the children were
teen-aged and they were a wonderful help.

But one evening Donald MacDougall said to his son, 'I think we'll go out tonight and do a bit of fishing.' Because it was a beautiful evening. And Mary filled a basket with all the things they would use, bait and hooks, and saw that her brother had everything he needed. Malcolm could row a boat as good as his daddy. And they didn't have any nets. It was all hand lines they fished with. Mary said good-bye to her brother and her daddy, and off they went fishing. Young Malcolm was rowing. But they went further than they usually went, because the fishing that night was really good. They went out for cod and anything else they could catch. The would dry their fish, hang them up for the winter. But the weather began to change.

Donald says to Malcolm, 'Malcolm, my son, I think we've gone a little farther than we should tonight. I think we should turn.' Being a fisherman he knew the weather. But then lo and behold they were caught in a storm. The most severe storm that ever happened blew up at that particular time.

And of course there were Mary and her mother at home thinking, 'Oh, they're caught in the storm. What will happen to them? I hope they'll be safe enough.' And they were out at the front of the house looking at the beach. Mary was watching for her brother and her daddy coming home. But the storm got so severe, so terribly wicked the boat overturned. Donald MacDougall had no fear for his son, because he was a great swimmer.

He says to him, 'Malcolm, swim for your life! Make for the shore. Forget the boat, forget everything! Let's save ourselves.' And Donald MacDougall was a great swimmer himself being a seaman. And he swam. The terrible storm blew. Donald MacDougall swam to the beach. When he came into the beach he stood up and looked all around. There was no sign of his son. His son was gone . . . His heart was broken! There was his wife Margaret and his daughter to meet him.

'And where is Malcolm? Is he not with you?' Malcolm was gone.

They searched the next day. And they searched far and wide. But Malcolm never turned up. He was lost at sea. Now they took a search party with many boats. Because word spread through the little village. They searched for his body but he never was found. A week passed. Two weeks passed. And then a strange thing began to happen to Mary.

She completely changed. She would sit there, would not talk to her parents. She would not look at them. She would not eat. She would pick at her food. She lost weight. She would not go to the village. All she would do was walk along the beach when she had spare time staring into the sea. And of course her parents were very worried about her. Their hearts were broken for their little son but they knew that he was gone. There was no chance they would ever find him because two weeks had passed. His body never was found. As for Mary, she became a changed girl. She crawled into her shell. She never helped her mother. She never talked to her father. She just sat around all day long staring at the floor. When she walked alone she would sit on the island — staring out to sea. The truth was, her heart was completely broken.

She could not go on with her life without her little brother whom she loved so dearly. But the days were to pass into weeks, the weeks were to pass into months. Her mother would go to the village. Daddy found his boat, and he was still going out fishing. But a big change had come over the family. Mary had become so much drawn into herself that she was completely lost to her parents. This upset them very much. Sometimes the parents would argue with each other during the night, which they had never done in their lives, and Mary would hear them. And she would lie there in her bed, rise in the morning, pick at her little bit of food and then be gone.

But the years passed by and this was the way she lived. She never went to the village. When her mother went to the shop she just stayed at home. She got so indrawn to herself she was just completely lost. But two years were to pass, two long years. Her parents thought they would bring in a doctor or psychiatrist or something. But Mary said, 'No, I don't want anything to do with them. Just leave me alone, leave me alone! Don't talk to me.' Till one day.

She took a walk along the beach. The tide was out. She walked the beach with her hair straying behind her staring into the sea. The tide was full out, the gulls were crying. She walked where she had walked many times before with her little brother. By this time she was sixteen years old. The beach was very clear, the sand was very soft along it. But further along, about a mile along the beach, the sand gave way to a lot of rocks. And then a cliff. In there was a cave where Mary had played many times with her little brother Malcolm. But she never visited it anymore. Then walking along the beach this evening she saw a strange thing in the sand. She saw marks coming out, as if a seal had come up onto the sand, soft sand. Then she stopped. When she saw the marks of the flippers in the sand she knew what it was, a seal had come out. But then there was a terrible change. The flipper marks gave way to foot marks, foot prints.

She followed the foot prints. But there was something strange about them as she looked. She followed them as they were quite plain in the soft sand. And just for curiosity she counted — one, two, three, four. On the right foot there were only four toes. Then she counted the left foot. And she saw one, two, three, four, five. She followed the foot prints gradually along the beach. She said, 'I wonder what this could be?' And she felt excitement in her heart. Something strange was taking place. Then she walked along the shore and along the shore. Then they stopped, because it came to rocks. But she still saw the wet marks on the rocks so she followed. And she climbed up over the rocks. Then she said, 'I'll go to the cave.' Something told her to go to the cave. When she went in she was in for the biggest surprise of her life. For sitting in the cave was a young man. She looked, and she saw, she stared. And she ran. He stood up. He threw his arms around her.

He says, 'Mary, my sister!'

'Malcolm, Malcolm,' she cried as the tears were streaming down her cheeks. 'You've come home. You've come back to me.'

'Yes sister,' he says, 'I've come back to you. But not for very long.'

'Oh Malcolm, Malcolm,' she said, 'where have you been all these years? Where have you been?' So he threw his arms around her and kissed her.

And he said, 'Sister, sit you down here.'

She says, 'You broke my heart. And you broke my parents' hearts. Why didn't you come home?'

He said, 'Mary, my dear sister, I couldn't come home.'

'Why didn't you come home? Why have you done this to me?

He said, 'I had no other choice.'

'Tell me,' she said, 'why is it you have done this to me?'

He said, 'I'll tell you. You remember that night I was caught in the storm with my daddy? And our boat capsized? Well, something happened to me. I seemed to get paralysed. I could not swim. And then, I felt something come and catch me, and put her arms around me . . . and she swam with me. Took me to the bottom of the sea. There she led me into a great passage. And there in a great cavern were all those people. You know how much I wanted to be a seal, Mary? How much I enjoyed the love of the seal people? Well, I became one of them.' And then she stood and looked.

'But,' she said, 'Malcolm, you're so tall. You're so fit!' He had grown tall, he had grown stout. And his dark hair was streaming down his back. And she looked at his hands. He put his hands around hers, and she saw that in between his fingers were like a duck's foot, with webbed fingers. Then she looked at his foot. She said, 'Malcolm, what's happened to you? Look at your foot!' For his big toe was gone.

'Well,' he said, 'Mary, my sister, you didn't like it very much.'

But she said, 'Why, Malcolm, why did you lose it?'

'Well,' he said, 'I'll tell you. When the seal people rescued me, and you know I love to be with them, I had to give them something of myself. Before I became one of them. And I knew you hated my big toe. So I gave them my toe, the only thing you didn't like about me.'

But she says, 'Malcolm, I didn't mean it, I didn't mean it!'

He says, 'It didn't hurt. They took it off. It didn't hurt! I feel fine without it.'

'Malcolm, come home! Mummy and daddy are dying to see you.'

He says, 'No, my dear, I can't come home to mummy and daddy tonight, or any other night. And I want you to make me a promise. You will never tell that you've seen me. Promise me right here and now you'll never tell you've seen me.'

She says, 'Malcolm, I promise. Will I see you again?'

He says, 'Mary, you'll see me many many times. But you must never, never tell my parents! Because you see I'm happy! This is the life I want. Now Mary, I must bid you good-bye. But I'll see you again. You know where to find me here.' And then they walked to the sea. He bade her good-bye and dived in.

But she stood there and watched. Sometimes when they were kids he would dive under the sea and he'd be gone for many minutes. She'd thought he was drowned. But this time she waited a few moments, and she thought he was not going to come up. But she looked. About ten yards out up came the head of a great big seal. It shook its head, and then was gone.

This was the happiest moment of Mary's life! She was completely transformed. Gone was the thought, gone was the worry, gone was everything. She hurried back, but she knew she would never tell her parents. When she walked into the house her mummy and daddy were sad, just sitting, and she was singing to herself. And her cheeks were rosy. Her parents looked . . . a strange thing had happened to Mary. She was singing! She was happy. Her face was flushed. She was standing straight. Her eyes were bright!

The parents looked and said, 'Mary has become a transformed girl all together!'

She said, 'Mummy, is the tea ready? Are you needing anything?'

This had never happened for two years. From that moment on Mary became a changed girl. She was back to her natural self. She could not do enough for her parents. She helped them in every way. The last two years had gone into the distance. Now she was sixteen years old. Once again she was happy. She sang at her work as she helped her mother and as she helped her father. She went to the village, talked to everyone. This, of course, made the parents very happy.

The thought of Malcolm was still in their minds. But seeing Mary like this changed everything for them. Their life began to renew itself. So life like that went on for many many years. Mary would go off on her long trips along the beach at night-time. Her mummy and daddy would say, 'She's off walking along the shore. She enjoys it.' But they looked when she came home. Every time she came back from her walks on the beach she was brighter, more happy, more handsome looking, more kind, more willing to help her parents. She helped her daddy in the fishing. She helped her mummy. But she always had those long walks. Now she would go to the village. She would go shopping for her mother. She would go to church with her parents. And by this time she was twenty years old. Another four years had passed by. Mary was the happiest girl in the whole place! She talked to everyone. She went to the dances. And many young men tried to woo Mary. But no way, she would not look at one single soul.

Mary became the happiest young woman in the whole village. And people talked and spoke but no one said an angry word against Mary. They often wondered why she never married. Because she was handsome, she was beautiful, she was kind. And she only had one friend whom she really respected more than anyone else — that was the local minister.

By this time Mary was thirty years old. And she still continued the same way of life. Naturally her parents were growing older, and now they were getting up in years Mary completely ruled the little croft. Her daddy stopped fishing. But Mary did fishing of her own. She brought enough back. She could handle a boat. She could do anything. She took care of the stock, did everything for them. And the parents depended on Mary. She would still go for her long walks in the evening. And she'd be gone for hours. Her mummy and daddy could not wait till they heard the click of the door. It was a little latch that opened the door. In the evening when she came back, Mary was smiling and happy. They never questioned her. But they knew wherever she went she was finding happiness. She was finding something that really made her happy. But unknown to them, Mary was visiting the cave on the cliff side. And there she spent most of her time with her brother. They had many long talks together. And he told her many wonderful things.

He told her about his life among the seal people. He told her how they transformed and became seal people down there. And how they walked on the land, how no one could recognise a seal person. Sometimes they walked in the village and saw the people going to church, but they always returned to the sea.

And of course Mary knew all this. But unknown to her parents she had a little red book at home, and she wrote down every single thing her brother had told her in this little diary. And this was the secret of hers. She had it hidden in her little room, in her bedroom. As I told you, she had one special friend, ten years younger than she, the local minister. He was only twenty. He took to the ministry when he was very young. And he lived with his parents. Even though he was a very young minister, he lectured in the church on Sunday.

Sometimes he would come for a visit. But they would sit there and talk in the house. They never walked together. Nothing was between them, just good friends. But then another ten years were to pass and Mary was forty years old, when, within a space of a year, both parents were gone. Some people said they broke their hearts over Malcolm. And of course Mary was left all alone. She never married. But she still went on her trips to the village. She brought eggs to the old people and she went to church. She went fishing. She became an old maid recluse, as we would call it on the West Coast. She lived by herself.

She sold every animal on the farm, never kept one single cat. No animals, no ducks, no hens. When her parents died she gave up everything, and the whole place went to grass. Her neighbours would graze their cattle or their sheep on her land. Sometimes the house would be locked up and she would be gone for weeks. No one knew where she went. Some said she was off on holiday. She had no stock to take care of. She just locked the door. Once a year she'd always for two weeks be gone. Maybe this was the reason she didn't keep any animals, because she'd go off on all these trips. Some people said she went to America, some said she went to Canada. But no one actually knew.

The years were to pass by. And Mary kept her own recluse way of life. An old maid. But she still kept in touch with the local minister. Mary never married, nor he never married. And his parents died. Her parents had been buried in a little cemetery with the little rough track going into the churchyard, just a muddy old road. Nice when the weather was dry, but when it was rain it got muddy. And people had to be very careful when they walked in the old graveyard. She visited it sometimes, the grave of her parents.

Then one day when Mary was sixty years old she never appeared in the village for two days. Of course the local friend of hers, the minister, got really worried. He took a walk down to visit Mary as all ministers do. He went to the door and knocked. The door was open. There was no one around and he walked in. He knocked on the bedroom.

A voice said, 'Come in. Who is it?' A very weak voice.

He said, 'It's me.' Robert was his name. 'Robert.'

She says, 'Come in, Robert, I'm in bed.' And he walked in there. By this time Mary was in her sixties, long grey hair, an old woman. She was lying in bed dressed in her night dress. She says, 'Robert, come sit down beside me!'

Robert came over and sat down by the bed. He said, 'What's wrong, Mary, with you?'

She says, 'Robert, I think my time has come. Look, I think I'm going to die. But I'm going to die happy.'

He says, 'Mary, you're not going to die — we'll take care of you! Are you feeling unwell?'

'No,' she said, 'I'm not feeling unwell. I know that my time has come. And I want to pass on. I'm sixty years of age now.' And he was fifty! Neither of the two of them were married. And of course in his own way he really loved her very much. She says, 'Robert, would you do something for me?'

He says, 'Yes, anything, Mary.'

She says, 'Reach under my pillow.' And he put his hand under the pillow and felt something. He brought it out. A little red book. She says, 'Robert, I won't be seeing you again.'

He says, 'What do you mean?'

She says, 'I won't be seeing you again. This is the last time we'll ever talk together. But I want you to do something for me.'

He says, 'Yes?'

'Well,' she says, 'look. I want you to take my little book. And I want you to read it. When I'm dead I want you to make me a promise. Everything I own is yours — I'm leaving it to the church. My parents have left me a lot of money. The land, the house — there's no one to own it but you. I'm giving it to you to sell it. I want you to give the money to the church, and share it with the old people. But I want you to promise me one thing. When I'm dead you'll put a little stone at my head.'

'Yes, Mary, of course. But you're not . . . '

She says, 'Robert, I know I'm going. I won't see you again. But I want you to give me your promise, and take my little book with you.' So he sat there and talked to her a long long time. And she says, 'All I'm asking you, Robert, is when I'm dead and buried in the little churchyard, I don't want to be buried with my parents. I want a little grave beside my parents. But I want you to find a little stone for me shaped like a heart. And I want you to put four words on that stone.'

'Of course, Mary,' he said, 'anything to please you.'

She says, 'Only four words, remember, nothing else! "To Malcolm and Mary".'

'I promise you.'

So she said, 'I think you'd better go now.' So the minister walked off sad at heart. She had given him a letter stating that everything she owned was to go to the church. And the little red book to the minister. Two days later Mary never appeared and they found she was dead. The minister saw that everything went according to the way she wanted it to be. Mary was laid to rest in a little grave not far from her parents. And the minister got a little stone carved in the shape of a heart. He put it at Mary's head. The four words said, 'To Malcolm and Mary'. And of course the place was sold. The minister collected all the money and it went to the church.

Now . . . that graveyard was to do the villagers for many years to come. The road was never mended for another fifty years. It was just a muddy path leading into the old, old grave- yard. And when people came to visit it, Mary's grave was near the gate. Her grave was always well kept. There were always wild flowers on her grave. But the most important thing of all was . . . it's so sad! Sometimes when the people walked on a Sunday after a heavy night's rain they had to walk by Mary's grave to see their relatives who were buried in the churchyard. And they saw something strange in the mud — the mark of two bare feet. The strange thing was one of the toes was missing from the foot mark. People wondered where the marks had come from. No one ever knew. Only one person knew, and that was the minister. He read that book many many times. And one evening he could not keep it to himself. So he told some of the villagers the story. He had to before he died. And of course one of the villagers was Angus MacNeil's grandmother. And before she died she told Angus the strange story of Seal Brother.

THE WOUNDED SEAL

*This silkie story was first told to me a long time ago in Argyll
by an old gamekeeper and deer stalker called Peter Munro. I
used to go with Peter sometimes when he took out his pony.
When he shot a deer out on the hill, a big stag, he would need
a help to lift the stag onto the back of the pony. He would
come by where I was working and ask the old farmer, 'Can
I borrow Duncan for an hour?' He would pay me half a
crown, and I always looked forward to this because it was
extra money. We were sitting resting one day when I asked
him about stories, and this is one he told me.*

TALES OF THE SEAL PEOPLE

IT ALL BEGAN A LONG TIME AGO on one of the islands off the north of Scotland. There lived a fisherman and his name was Duncan MacKinnon. And Duncan was a good fisherman. His parents had died and left him a large house, a large piece of land and some money. But Duncan was more of a hunter than a fisherman. For he liked to hunt the seals. He would kill them on the little island where he lived, take the skins home, stretch them out, salt and stretch them and leave the bodies of the seals lying in the sea to rot. And he preferred this. Now there were no restrictions against killing seals back in that long bygone time, and Duncan was famed as a seal killer. Everybody bought his skins, for they were in a great demand.

But there was one thing Duncan MacKinnon would not touch — a young seal, not even a half-grown seal. Whether he thought to himself, 'I'll leave them till they grow bigger and I'll have a bigger skin,' or whether he really felt sorry for the younger seals, he felt some pity because they were young, I don't know. But he never killed a young seal of any kind. He always went for the old ones.

And he used to wait till they were lying sunning themselves on the island not far from where he lived. And he only carried a knife, no gun, no stick, just a big long knife. He'd crawl up, get as close to the seal as he could while the seal was sunning itself. Dive on the seal and stick the knife in its neck, kill it. Then he would skin it and throw the body of the seal into the sea.

Now through the years he'd collected and sold many skins. Then for some strange reason people stopped buying his skins. And he had a large collection of skins. He was wondering what he was going to do with them. But he still continued to kill the seals and collect them up.

It was near the beginning of winter time, and it was a terrible stormy night. He was sitting in his house by the peat fire smoking his pipe when he heard a knock on the door. He wondered to himself, 'Who could this be?' Because he didn't get very many visitors. Only when he walked to the village and had a drink in the pub would he have a news with the rest of the folk. Not many people came a-calling as late as this. It was

100

around ten o'clock. He thought to himself, 'I wonder who this could be.'

He went to the door and he opened it. In this strange dark light in front of the house he saw a tall, dark stranger with a long, dark coat reaching to his feet with his neck buried in the collar of the long, dark, black coat.

The stranger spoke in a kind of Highland accent, 'Are you Duncan MacKinnon? The seal hunter?'

'I am. Can I help you?' said Duncan.

He said, 'Yes, you can. Have you any sealskins for sale?'

'At the moment,' he said, 'I have.'

'Well,' he said, 'I have someone waiting to buy every one from you. Would you sell them to him?'

'Oh,' Duncan said, 'well, I have plenty skins to sell. Where is your friend?'

He said, 'He didn't come down, he's kind of tired. We walked a long way. He's sitting on the top of the cliff.' Now there was a large, deep, deep cliff not far from where Duncan lived. He said, 'It's not far away.'

Duncan said, 'I know the place well.'

'Well,' he said, 'if you'd like to walk up and have a talk to him, I think he'll buy all your skins from you.'

Duncan had never seen this stranger before in his life. And he'd never heard such a strange mixed accent of a voice. It was neither Gaelic nor English. It was in between both. So he says, 'Just a moment, I'll get my coat.' He got his coat and he came out. By this time the storm had calmed.

The stranger said, 'All right, are you ready?'

He said, 'I'm ready.'

'Let's walk then,' he said. So they walked along the pathway that led to the cliff. And Duncan could barely keep up with the stranger with his long, strange strides he was taking. He could see he was very tall, and he looked powerfully built. He must have been six feet tall. And he was striding on with this long coat. Duncan looked down at his feet in the fading light and he could see he had long, black socks up under the coat. Strong, thick, heavy boots. Duncan wondered where he could come from.

He said to himself, 'He looks like a rich man. And if his

friend is as rich as he looks, he'll be able to buy all my skins!' This is what he was looking forward to.

So they walked together, went up the cliff. And the moon was under the clouds, and the clouds were passing by. There was a breeze blowing. It was kind of cold, it was kind of dark. And kind of misty. And they walked up the cliff. Duncan had walked it many times. He'd never actually been at the top, but he knew where it was. So they climbed. And when they came to the top of the cliff, it was high — a deep drop nearly five hundred feet into the sea below. And when the tide was full in it was very, very deep.

The stranger stopped. He said, 'Are you there?' There was no answer. Duncan stood behind him. He said louder, 'Are you there? Friend?' There was no answer. And then he turned round to Duncan and he said, 'He seems to have wandered off some- where. I wonder where he can be.' Then he came up as close to the cliff edge as he could. And he said, 'Doesn't it look deep down there? Do you see anything down there? Maybe he's fallen in.' And Duncan came up close to the edge and looked over. Just the moment he did that the stranger put his arm around him — and they dived into the sea!

Down and down and down they went with a splash. And then he felt a hand going around his mouth! Down into the deep . . . and down and down they went. And he could see the stranger was a powerful swimmer, for as they went down and down he could feel the stranger's hand holding his mouth. Till his lungs were bursting. And he was choking for a breath of air. But down went the stranger. And then he felt his feet turning, touching bottom. The stranger's arm was still around him. And gasping for a breath — he was about to choke for the want of air — when he was led into a passageway under the sea, through to the face of the cliff. And he gasped for air — the stranger took his hand away from his mouth. They were in a long tunnel under the cliff. And he had a strong grip on his arm. He said, 'Duncan MacKinnon, come with me! I want you to meet my friends.'

Duncan wondered, 'What could this be?'

And he half pulled Duncan, half led him through a long dark tunnel. Then they saw a light ahead. In the light was a great cavern. And all those flares on the walls, flares blazing. Duncan could see that the whole cavern was lit up. Then to his amazement he looked and saw all these people sitting around on these kind of stone chairs. There were old people, young people, all dressed in black, all looking the same with their brown eyes. They were staring straight at him as he was marched in between the whole group. There were old men, there were young people, there were women sitting with babies wrapped in black cloths on their backs. But no one said one single word. They just sat and stared. And there was a fire burning in the centre of the cavern. He was led up to the fire.

Then the man spoke, 'I have him.' Then all the men rose. The women sat still. The men came up and Duncan could see every one's arm held a big long knife!

And he said, 'Oh, my God, I'm going to be killed! What have I done?'

Then the stranger turned round and he pulled down the neck of his coat. Duncan could see he had dark eyebrows, he had dark brown eyes. And he said, 'Duncan MacKinnon, I have brought you here. You see, you have been killing our people.'

'People?' says Duncan. 'I-I-I've never killed anyone in my life.'

He said, 'You've been killing our people, our seal people. And we have brought you here!'

Duncan thought, 'I'm going to be killed. This is the end for me. Who are these people? Where have they come from?'

And the stranger said, 'Yesterday you did something terrible. You stabbed my father. But he was lucky he escaped. Now come with me!' And he led him through a little passage in the cavern. There on a stone bench lay an old man with long grey hair. And his face was pale, his eyes were closed. And stuck in his shoulder was Duncan's big knife! For Duncan had wrestled a seal the day before and the seal was so powerful that he'd escaped with Duncan's knife still in his back. And the tall stranger said, 'Is that your knife?'

Duncan said, 'Yes, it's my knife.'

'Well,' he said, 'that's my father! Come with me.' He led him over. The old man was lying on his mouth and nose like this, with his head twisted to the side. And he could see that the coat had been split down the back of his neck and there was a great big wound. It was full of pus, and the knife was still stuck in it. And the tall stranger said to him, 'Duncan MacKinnon, pull out that knife!'

Duncan reached over and he pulled out the knife. He saw that there were pus and blood sticking to the knife.

'Now,' he said, 'that's what you've done to my father. But there's one thing, Duncan MacKinnon, you have never done. That we appreciate a little, but not much — you have never killed any of our children. And for that we are going to give you a chance. I want you to go and kiss that wound that's on my father's shoulder.' He had no other choice!

So Duncan walked over. He reached over — and the smell of the pus of the thing with his nostrils he could feel — the big bloody wound.

'Go on,' said the stranger, 'kiss it!'

And Duncan leaned over for he had no other choice, for the peril of his life — and he kissed the wound of the old man's shoulder — and just like that a strange thing happened. For as he kissed the wound on the old man's shoulder the old man turned round and his eyes lighted up.

And he said, 'Thank you, Duncan!' He sat up. 'Now' he said, 'Duncan MacKinnon, for what you've done, we're going to give you one more chance.' Not another soul said a word. The old man, he stood up. The look of pain had left his face. His eyes were bright. They walked back to the fire and the old man heated his hands. He said, 'Bring me a bag!'

And Duncan stood there, he thought he was going to be killed. And one of the young men rushed over and came back with a leather bag. He passed it to the old man. The old man felt it and he weighed it in his hands. And he says, 'Duncan MacKinnon, take this! In the future do some good to the seals. Do them no harm!'

And the tall stranger said, 'Then, Duncan MacKinnon, you'd better come with me. And hang on to that bag!' They never laid a finger on him. All the people stood and stared as he marched away. Not one woman spoke, not one child. Only two people and the old man had spoken. He led him back through the passage again to the end of the tunnel. And then he put his arm around Duncan's neck once again, hand across his mouth and said, 'Hang on to that bag!' They swam upwards. And Duncan gasped for breath — just then his head appeared above the surface. And the great powerful stranger swam to the shore, and he pulled Duncan on to the rocks.

'Now,' he said, 'Duncan MacKinnon, remember, do something good for the seals in the future!' And he was gone.

Duncan climbed up onto the shore. And he hurried home. He's still hanging on for dear life to this bag! And he could feel that it was heavy. But he went inside, he was soaking wet. He put the bag on the table. He was trembling with fear. The first thing he did, he rushed and filled himself a glass of whisky. And his hands were shaking. And he drank the whisky. He was lucky to be alive he thought to himself. And when he had put dry clothes on he sat by the fireside to heat himself for a little while. The fire was still burning brightly. He took the bag made of leather and he emptied it on the table. It was full of hundreds of thousands of gold pieces of all sizes!

Duncan said, 'What has happened to me? This is amazing.' And then he thought to himself, 'I will never touch a seal again as long as I live.' And he took the Bible, put it on his knee, and he swore to himself in the future he would never touch another seal. Anything he ever did again would be for the good of the seals and for the good of the seals only.

So three days later Duncan sold his house and sold everything he owned and he moved off to another island. There he bought a large piece of land, with an island into it, where seals lived. And he built himself a house on it. He spent the rest of his life protecting those seals, to see that no one would touch them so they could live in peace. And some people say that that part of the island today is on the Isle of Skye. Duncan MacKinnon lived to be an old man and he never touched another seal as long as he lived. And that's the end of my story.

SEAL HOUSE

When I ran away from school at the age of thirteen I was so in love with stories that I thought to myself, because my father and my Aunt Rachel had told me so many fishing stories, there must be a terrible lot among the fishing people. I went west from Furnace to Kintyre and spent two years on the West Coast with the crofting community. I learned so many beautiful stories around by Kintyre, around the lear side up by Kilberry, round by Lochgilphead and down by Bellanoch, finding a wee bit job and searching for stories with a lot of sea and crofting people. But their people, some had come from the Western Isles and had brought with them family stories, silkie tales. This one was told to me by an old fisherman, and he said, 'That is a true story.' It happened over a hundred years ago, maybe a little more.

TALES OF THE SEAL PEOPLE

AN OLD CROFTING MAN HAD TWO SONS. He had a small croft, and like all the rest of the crofters he did not have much arable land. He kept a few sheep and a few goats, and only enough animals that could survive on this small piece of land he owned. But his two sons could not survive by working the land, so their father bought them a boat. They would have to make a living from the sea the best they could. Fish for lobsters or crabs, or they could get themselves a net and fish, sell the fish in the market. But they were not the only ones. There were many who turned to the sea to make a living. Now there was no limit against killing seals in these bygone days for their skins. There were thousands and hundreds of seals in all the little rocks and bays along the West Coast. And of course people thought, these seals are taking our food from us. There's too many of them anyway. The fishermen would go out on a cull.

So this one evening a seal cull had been arranged. The fishing was getting poor. There was a big demand for sealskins. They were the finest things for making bagpipe bags in these days. Producers of bagpipes would buy all the sealskins, as many as could be found. So a few friends from neighbouring crofts got together. Six of them. They would go out to Seal Island. Just a barren island where the seals lived. Some men came from three and four miles away for the cull. They got together, just like going to a ceilidh.

For the seals it had been a beautiful sunny day. And the plan for the cull was to go in the evening, when the seals would lie in the late sunshine after feeding all day long. The boat would pull in at one end of the island. The men would creep round the island, two would come from the north, two would come from the east, two would come from the west. They would try and trap the seals in the middle. The seals would be basking on the rocks, enjoying the heat from the stones and the heat from the sun. Seals love sunshine! They would have their bellies full of fish and lie there till they got hungry. Some would be asleep. They would hardly ever hear the boat coming in. Quietly. Of course, if the seals tried to run this way or that once the men were around them, there would always be two men to knock them over. With their clubs. Beat the brains out of the seals.

Kill as many as they could while the other ones escaped into the sea. And maybe that night they would kill a dozen. Now a dozen sealskins shared between six of them would be a good day's wages. So it was arranged. The men had a few drams together. They sat, they talked and they waited for the long evening sun.

But not far from Seal Island a businessman a long time ago had built himself a big house, a two-storey house, from bricks or stones. But there he lived by himself. No one knew where he came from. Some people said he was a foreigner. But he didn't mix with the local people. He was known as 'the foreigner'. It was called the Foreigner's House. He'd built this beautiful house on the far shore and a large driveway leading up to it. But this was across from the island, and across the sea loch. After a few years, whatever happened, he seemingly gave up. The foreigner moved away. Whether he came from Russia or from Germany no one actually knew. The foreigner left the large house. He gave it to no one. No one lived in that house any more. And as the years passed on, the house became derelict. The windows got broken with the gales. The doors were unpainted. The Foreigner's House lay vacant for many years.

But these six young men that evening took their boat after they had a good drink, and they rowed out to the island. They knew there were many seals there that night. They came in quietly to Seal Island. And lo and behold there were the seals lying. But the moment they landed on the island every seal vanished! All the seals, as if they had been forewarned, jumped into the sea. There was not one single seal they could capture or strike that night. And the six of them gathered in the middle of the island and stood there.

They said, 'What's happened? We've never seen this before.' They stood in a semi-circle, they lighted cigarettes. Some smoked pipes. And then, down at that very moment, even though it had been a beautiful sunny evening — came the mist! Now this island was known for the mist, but it had never come at this time of the year. But within a few moments, just as they stood there, the whole island was blackened with mist. They had come about two miles from the mainland to this island. And you know rowing a boat in thick fog or mist is a hard job!

They stood and talked, they talked and talked. And the mist got thicker and thicker and thicker.

They said to each other, 'What's gone wrong? What's happened? What's going on here?' They'd never seen this before. There was not a seal in sight. 'Well,' they said, 'we'll have to make our way home to the mainland.' So it was a long clinker-built wooden boat. It would hold up to about twelve people. There were three rowing and three sitting at the back. They pulled out into the sea. But the mist was so thick you could barely see your finger before you. It got dark. They had stayed longer on the island than they'd meant to waiting for the mist to clear. Now darkness came along as well. They didn't know which direction to take. Then they looked across. They saw the lights.

So they pulled further out into the sea. But at that moment they were surrounded by seals! The seals came from all directions. And some of them were around the boat and climbing on the boat. They were pushing the boat, trying to flip to get into the boat. Trying to cowp it the best way they would with these six men in the boat. The men were in a terrible problem. Now seals as a rule don't get together, only once in a year has anyone ever seen a seal gathering. Seals like to keep by themselves. But this was the largest collection of seals the men had ever seen in all their lives. They nearly overpowered the boat. The men of course got their oars and stopped rowing, started punching the seals. These seals were going to cowp the boat, put them in the sea, a long way from the mainland! But then up from behind the boat came an old bull seal. And the men could see that he was very old. He had put his flippers across the boat. And the weight of him was pushing the boat down. One of the men took his oar and he hit the old seal in the mouth. And he knocked all his teeth out. And he saw the blood. It disappeared in the sea. And then every seal was gone. So they rowed around in circles and circles in the dark, in the fog. Then they saw a light again.

'Let's make for the light, boys!' they cried. So they rowed for the light. They beached the boat. But they were far away from the village. Where were the lights coming from — the old Foreigner's House! They said, 'It must be somebody's taken over the house. Maybe they'll give us shelter. Maybe they'll give us a dram. We'll wait till daylight.' So they made their way up the beach to the old Foreigner's House that had been derelict for many years. But when they landed there, the house was in a lunary of lights! The whole house was lighted. So they knocked on the door. And the door opened.

This tall dark man with a long dark coat said, 'Hello, come on in! Make yourselves at home!'

They all came in, one by one, six of them. There was a table. There were bottles of drink, liquid laid in the middle of the table. And all those people around against the wall. Strangers they had never seen. But everyone was dressed the same way. Long dark coats. There were old people, young people. There were teenagers, young women, there were old women. There must have been over a hundred of them. And they were all sitting around the room. Of course these fishermen had never seen the likes of this before in their lives. They lined up against the wall.

So the spokesman for the whole crowd said, 'Be seated! Welcome, gentlemen, to our home. But we can not do anything till Grandfather comes. You can enjoy yourselves. You can have as much to drink as you like, but we'll have to wait on Grandfather.'

These men were terrified. They'd never seen these strange people before. No one was recognisable, everyone was looking very, very strange. The women with these burning brown eyes. These fishermen were afraid. Some of the people were standing, some were sitting, some sitting around the table.

Then they said, 'Gentlemen, we'd like to give you something to drink, but we'll have to wait on Grandfather.' They sat there for a few minutes. They didn't know what to do. They knew in their own minds this was the Foreigner's House. It had been derelict for many years. Where did these people come from? They were not local villagers. They were not crofters. And there was a stair leading down in the middle of the house. Down the stair comes an old man with a long grey beard.

They all cried, 'Grand-dad, Grandfather, come here! We've someone to show you. We have something to show you.' And these six fishermen were lined against the wall. And Grandfather

111

came down. They could see that his beard was tainted red with blood. And when he came to the middle of the room he looked round.

'Oh,' he said, 'these are the ones.' And he opened his mouth, and all his front teeth were knocked out! His gums were red with blood. He says, 'Kill them!' And every one around the room drew their knives. Long knives from under their coats, from under their jackets, from anywhere. And these fishermen they stood terrified. The one who was near the door put his back against it. He opened the door carefully with his hand.

He said, 'Boys, let's go! Run for your lives!' And one after one they ran out of that house. There were screams and shouts. But no one followed them. They ran to their boat. They jumped in and they rowed back. By this time the mist had cleared. They knew where they were going — home! And these men were terrified as they rowed that boat home that night across the sea loch from the Foreigner's House. And when they landed on the beach and pulled the boat up they stood together.

They said, 'What happened? Who were these people?'

'Let's go home tonight,' one said. 'We'll find out tomorrow.'

So they all split up and went to their homes. But they could not rest. Some sat, some drank, some fell asleep. Some went home to their old wives, some did not go. But the next morning they made a pact they would find the truth. When the sun was shining there was nothing to be afraid of. Six of them with guns rowed back across the sea loch to the Foreigner's House. Pulled the boat on the beach up on the shore, with shot guns and everything else they marched up! Who were these foreigners who were in the old house? They were going to find the truth. Who terrified them, nearly caused them their deaths? But when they walked up to the house the door was hanging on its hinges. The windows were full of cobwebs. The floor was full of dust. There was no one there. They searched the house up and they searched the house down.

And the spokesman of the group, an old crofting man said, 'Boys, look, I'll tell you something. Look, we have come in contact with the seal people. I think it would be better if we leave these people alone. Because my grandmother used to tell me many many stories. I think we have killed too many seals.'

SEAL HOUSE

And from that day on not another one of these six people ever killed another seal for their skins. And that's the end of my story.

MARY AND THE SEAL

This is a Gaelic tale from the Western Isles. The story was told to me when I was only about fifteen years of age, doing the stone-dyking in Argyll at Auchindrain with a mason, Mr Neil MacCallum. He was a crofter, his brother was a crofter. And, just to sit there listening . . . I can still hear his voice in my ears; you know, his voice is still there after, maybe, nearly forty years. And every little detail is imprinted in my memory. And when I tell you the story, I try to get as close as possible to the way that he spoke to me.

MANY YEARS AGO in a little isle off the West Coast of Scotland — it could be Mull, Tiree, or any island — there lived an old fisherman and his wife. And the old fisherman spent his entire life fishing in the sea and selling whatever fish he couldn't use himself to keep him and his wife and his little daughter alive. They lived in this little cottage by the sea and not far from where they stayed was the village, a very small village — a post office, a hall and some cottages. But everyone knew everyone else. And his cousin also had a house in the village.

This old man and woman had a daughter called Mary and they loved her dearly, she was such a nice child. She helped her father with the fishing and when she was finished helping her father, she always came and helped her mother to do housework and everything else. The father used to set his nets every day in the sea and he used to rise early every morning. Mary used to get up and help her father lift his nets and collect the fish. After that was done she used to help her mother, then went off to school. Everybody was happy for Mary. And her father and mother were so proud of her because she was such a good worker. But she was such a quiet and tender little girl and didn't pay attention to anyone . . . she did her schoolwork in school. The years passed by and Mary grew till she became a young teenager.

This is where the story really begins, when Mary was about sixteen or seventeen. She always used to borrow her father's boat, every evening in the summertime, and go for a sail to a little island that lay about half a mile from where they stayed, a small island out in the middle of the sea-loch. And Mary used to go out and spend all her spare time on the island. Every time she'd finished her day's work with her father and helped her mother and had her supper, she would say, 'Father, can I borrow your boat?' Even in the wintertime sometimes, when the sea wasn't too rough, she would go out there and spend her time. Her father and mother never paid any attention because Mary's spare time was her own time; when her work was finished she could do what she liked. Till one day.

Her mother used to walk down to the small village to the post office where they bought their small quantity of messages and did their shopping, it was the only place they could buy any supplies. She heard two old women nattering to each other. Mary's mother's back was turned at the time but she overheard the two old women. They were busy talking about Mary.

'Och,' one woman said, 'she's such a nice girl, but she's so quiet. She doesn't come to any of the dances and she doesn't even have a boyfriend. She doesn't do anything — we have our ceilidhs and we have our things and we never see her come, she never even pays us a visit. Such a nice quiet girl, all she wants to do, she tells me, is to take her boat and she rows over to the island and spends all her time there on the island. Never even comes and has a wee timey — when our children have their shows and activities in school she never puts in an appearance! And her mother and father are such decent people . . . even her Uncle Lachy gets upset!'

This was the first time her mother had heard these whispers so she paid little attention. She came home, and she was a wee bit upset. And the next time she went back to the village she heard the same whispers again — this began to get into her mind, she began to think. But otherwise Mary was just a natural girl: she helped her daddy and she asked her mummy if there was anything she could do, helped her to do everything in the house, and she was natural in every way. But she kept herself to herself.

One evening it was suppertime once more, and after supper Mary said, 'Daddy, can I borrow your boat?'

'Oh yes, Mary, my dear,' he said, 'you can borrow the boat. I'm sure I'm finished — we've finished our day's work. You can have the boat.' It wasn't far across to row the little boat, maybe several hundred yards to the wee island in the loch. And the old woman and the old man sat by the fire.

Once Mary had walked out the door and said good-bye to her father and mother, the old woman turned round and said to her husband, 'There she goes again. That's her gone again.'

Mary's father turned round and he said, 'What do you mean? Margaret, what do you mean — you know Mary always goes off, an-and-and enjoys herself in the boat.'

She said, 'Angus, you don't know what I mean: it's not you that has got to go down to the village and listen to the whispers of the people, and the talk and the wagging tongues.'

He says, 'Woman, what are you talking about?'

She says, 'I'm talking about your daughter.'

Angus didn't know what to say . . . he said, 'What's wrong with my daughter? I'm sure she works hard and she deserves a little time by herself — what's the trouble, was there something that you needed done that she didn't do?'

'Not at all,' she said, 'that's not what I'm talking about.'

'Well,' he says, 'tell me what you're trying to say!'

She said, 'Angus, it's Mary — the people in the village are beginning to talk.'

'And what are they saying,' he said, 'about my daughter!' And he started to get angry.

'They're talking about Mary going off herself in her boat to the island and spending all her time there, she's done that now for close on five years. And they say she doesn't go to any dances, she doesn't go to any parties and she doesn't accept any invitations to go anywhere and she has no boyfriend! And the wagging tongues in the village are talking about this. It's getting through to me and I just don't like it.'

'Well,' he said, 'Mother, I'm sure there's nothing in the world that should upset you about that; I'm sure Mary's minding her own business! And if she's out there, she's no skylarking with some young man — would you rather have her skylarking around the village with some young man or something? And destroying herself and bringing back a baby or something to you — would you enjoy that better?'

'It's not that, Angus,' she said, 'it's just that Mary is so unsociable.'

But anyway, they argued and bargued for about an hour and they couldn't get any further. By the time they were finished Mary came in again. She was so radiant and happy.

She came over, kissed her mother and kissed her daddy, said, 'Daddy, I pulled the boat up on the beach, and everything's all right.'

He says, 'All right, Daughter, that's nice.'

'And,' she says, 'Daddy, the tide is coming in and some of the corks of the net are nearly sunk, so I think we'll have a good fishing in the morning. I'll be up bright and early to give you a hand.'

He said, 'Thank you, Mary, very much.'

And she kissed her mother and said, 'I'll just have a small something to eat and I'll go to bed.'

But anyway, the old woman was unsettled. 'There she goes again,' she says, 'that's all we get.'

'Well,' he says, 'what more do you expect? She's doing her best, Mother. She's enjoying herself.'

'What is she doing on that island? That's what I want to know.'

Said the old man to Margaret, 'Well, she's no doing any harm out there.'

So the next morning they were up bright and early, had their breakfast. And Mary went out with her father, collected the nets, collected the fish, and they graded the fish and kept some for themselves. Then they went into the village and sold the rest, came back home, had their supper. It was a beautiful day.

And Mary said, 'Is there anything you want me to do, Mother?'

'Well no, Mary,' she says, 'everything is properly done. The washing's finished and the cleaning's finished, and I was just making some jam; and I'm sure your father's going to sit down and have a rest because he's had a hard day.'

Mary turned round and she said, 'Father, could I borrow your boat?' once again.

'I'm sure, my dear,' he says, 'you can have the boat. Take the boat. Now be careful because there might be a rise of a storm.'

'I'll be all right, Father,' she said, 'I don't think it's going to — the sky looks so quiet and peaceful. I doubt if we'll have a storm the night.' And away she goes.

But as soon as she takes off in the boat, oh, her mother gets up. 'That's it, there she goes again,' she said. 'To put my mind at rest, would you do something for me?'

Angus said, 'What is it you want now, woman?'

'Look,' she said, 'would you relieve my mind for me: would you go down and borrow Lachy's boat, your cousin Lachy's boat, and row out to the island and see what Mary does when she goes there? It'll put my mind at rest.'

'That's no reason for me to go out,' he said. 'Let the lassie enjoy herself if she wants to enjoy herself! There's no reason

119

for me to go out — I'm sure there's no-one within miles. Maybe she's wading on the beach and she sits there, an-and-and maybe she has some books with her, and she — she likes to be by herself.'

But no. She says, 'Look, do something for me, husband! Would you go out, Angus, and see what she does?'

So Angus said, 'Och, dash it, woman! To keep you happy, I'll go out and see what she's doing. It's only a waste of time anyway.'

So he walks down; it was only about two hundred yards down to Lachy's cottage. Lachy had the same kind of boat. He was sitting at the fire; he had never married; their fathers had been brothers. Lachy stayed in this cottage, he was an old retired seaman and he always liked to keep a boat.

'Well, it's yourself, Angus!' he said. 'Come away in. And come you, sit down and we'll have a wee dram.'

'No,' he said, 'Angus, I'm not here for a dram.'

'Well,' he said, 'what sent you down? It's not often you come for a visit.'

'I was wondering,' he said, 'if you would let me borrow your boat for a few minutes?'

And Lachy said, 'Well, what's the trouble?'

'Ach, it's no trouble, really,' he said, 'I was just wanting to borrow your boat for maybe half an hour or so.'

'Well, what is wrong with your own boat?'

'Och,' he said, 'Mary's using it.'

And Lachy said, 'Och, that's Mary off on her gallivant to the island again. And you want to follow the lassie and see what she's doing. If I was you I would leave her alone. Come on, sit down and have a dram with me and forget about it.'

But old Angus was so persistent, 'I want to borrow your boat.'

'Well,' he said, 'take the dashit thing and away you go!'

He takes the boat and he rows across to the island and he lands on the small beach. There was Mary's boat beached. And he pulls his cousin Lachy's boat up beside Mary's, and beaches it. And he walks up a path — it was well worn because Mary had walked up this path many many times — he follows the path up, goes over a little knowe. There are some rocks and a few trees, and down at the back of the island is a small kind of valley-shaped place that leads out to the sea. Then there's a beach, on the beach is a large rock. And beside the rock is a wee green patch.

Old Angus came walking up, taking his time — looked all around and looked all around. There were a few seagulls flying around and a few birds wading along the beach because the tide was on the ebb. And he heard the laughing coming on. Giggling and laughing — this was Mary, carrying on. And he came up over the knowe, he looked down — here was Mary — with a large seal, a grey seal. And they were having the greatest fun you've ever seen: they were wrestling in the sand, carrying on and laughing, the seal was grunting and Mary was flinging her arms around the seal!

So Angus stopped, he sat down and watched for a wee while. He said, 'Ach, I'm sure she's doing no harm, it's only a seal. And her mother was so worried about it. She's enjoying herself; probably she's reared it up from a pup and she comes over to feed it, and I'm sure it won't do her any harm. She's better playing with a seal than carrying on with a young bachle as far as I'm concerned!'

So, he takes his boat and he rows home, gives his cousin Lachy back the boat, lights his pipe and walks up to his own home. He comes in through the door and his old wife, old Margaret, is waiting on him.

She said, 'You're home, Angus.'

'Aye, I'm home,' he said, 'Margaret, I'm home. And thanks be praised to God I am home!'

She said, 'Did you see Mary?'

'Of course,' he said, 'I saw Mary. She's out on the island.'

'And what is she doing? Is she sitting — what is she doing?'

He said, 'She's enjoying herself.'

Old Margaret said, 'What way is she enjoying herself — is she wading on the beach or something?'

'No,' he said, 'she's not wading on the beach.'

'Is she reading?'

'No, she's not reading.' He said, 'She's playing herself with a seal.'

She said, 'What did you say?'

He said, 'She's playing herself — she has the best company in the world and she's enjoying herself — she's playing with a seal! A large grey seal. They're having great fun and I didn't interfere.'

She said, 'Angus, Mary's enchanted. It's one of the sea-people that's taken over. Your daughter is finished — ruined for evermore. I've heard stories from my grandmother how the sea-people take over a person and take them away for evermore, they're never seen again — she's enchanted. What kind of a seal was it?'

He said, 'It was a grey seal and they were having good fun so I didn't interfere.'

She said, 'If you want to protect your daughter and you want to have your daughter for any length of time, you'd better get rid of the seal.'

He says, 'Margaret, I couldn't interfere with them. It's Mary's pet.'

'I don't care if it's Mary's pet or no,' she said, 'tomorrow morning you will take your gun and go out, instead of going to the fish you'll go out and you'll shoot that seal and destroy if for evermore!'

'But,' he said, 'it's Mary's pet — she probably reared it up unknown to us, she probably reared it up from a young pup, and it's not for me to destroy the seal, the thing she has to play with.'

'I'm sure she can find plenty of company in the village instead of going out there to the island!'

But the argument went on, and they argued and argued and finally old Margaret won. He lighted his pipe to have a smoke before going to bed.

'Well,' he said, 'in the morning I'll go out and see.'

Then Mary came home and she was so radiant and so bright, so happy. She came in and kissed her daddy and kissed her mummy. She had a cup of tea and asked Mummy and Daddy if they needed anything or wanted anything done.

And they said, 'No, Mary.'

The old woman was a wee bit kind of dubious. She wasn't just a wee bit too pleased. And Mary saw this.

She said, 'Is there something wrong, Mother?'

'No, Mary,' she said, 'there's nothing wrong.'

'Well, I'm going off to my bed.' Mary went to her bed. In these cottages in times long ago in the little crofts, the elderly people stayed down on the floor and there was a small ladder that led up to the garret in the roof. If you had any children they had their beds in the garret. Mary lived upstairs.

So the next morning Angus got up early. And before he even had any breakfast, he went ben the back of the house and took his gun. He loaded his gun and took his boat and he rowed out to the island, before Mary was up. And he walked up the path, the way Mary usually went, over the little hillock, down the little path to the little green part beside the bare rock — sure enough, sitting there sunning himself in the morning sun was the seal.

Angus crept up as close as he could — he fired the shot at the seal, hit the seal. And the seal just reared up — fell, and then crawled, made its way into the sea, hobbled its way into the water and disappeared. 'That's got you,' he said.

And then he felt queer. A funny sensation came over him. And he sat down, he felt so funny — as if he had shot his wife or his daughter. A sadness came over him. And he sat for a long while, then he left the gun down beside him and he looked at the gun . . . he felt that he had done something terrible. He felt so queer.

So he picked up the gun, walked back to his boat and he could barely walk, he felt so sick. He put the gun in the boat. He sat for a while before he could even take off in the boat and he had the queer sensation, a feeling of loss was within him, a terrible feeling of loss — that something he had done could never be undone . . . he could hardly row the boat. But he finally made his way back to the mainland, tied up his boat, picked up the gun, and put it back in the cupboard. He walked in and old Margaret was sitting there.

She said, 'You're back, Angus.'

He said, 'Yes I'm back.'

She said, 'Did you do what I told you to do?'

'Yes, Mother,' he said, 'I did what you — what you told me to do.'

She said, 'Did you see the seal?'

'Yes,' he said, 'I saw the seal. And I shot the seal.'

She sat down. 'Are you wanting . . . '

'No, I don't want any breakfast,' he said.

She says, 'Are you feeling . . . '

'No, I'm not feeling very well. I'm not feeling very well at all.'

She says, 'What's wrong with you?'

'Well,' he says, 'I feel terrible, I feel queer and I feel so kind of sad . . . I've done something wrong and you forced me to it, I hope in the future that you'll be sorry for it.'

'Och,' she said, 'it's only a seal!'

But they said no more. By this time Mary had come down.

She said, 'Good morning, Father; good morning, Mother,' and she sat down at the table as radiant as a flower and had some breakfast. 'Are you not eating, Daddy?'

'No,' he said, 'Daughter, I don't . . . '

She said, 'Are you not feeling well?' And she came over and stroked her father's head. 'Are you not feeling very well, Father?'

'Oh,' he said, 'I'm feeling fine, Mary. I'm just not, just — what I should be.'

And the mother tried to hide her face in case Mary could see something in her face that would — a give away in her face, you know.

'Well,' she says, 'Father, are you ready to go out to lift the net?'

'Well, Mary, to tell you the truth,' he said, 'I don't think the tide'll be on the — the out-going tide won't be for a while yet. No, I think I'll sit here and have a smoke.'

'Mother,' she says, 'are you needing anything done?'

'No, Mary,' she said, 'we don't need anything done.'

Now they wanted to try and be as canny with her as possible. They didn't want to upset her in any way.

And the mother said, 'No, Mary, I think everything's done. There's only a little cleaning to be done and I think I'll manage.'

Mary says, 'Well, after I milk the cow, Father, would it be all right if I take the boat?'

'Och, yes, Daughter, go ahead and help yourself to the boat,' he said, 'I'm sure you can have the boat any time. You don't need to ask me for the boat, just take it whenever you feel like it.'

So Mary milked the cow, brought in the milk and set the basins for the cream, and did everything that was needing to be done. She said, 'Goodbye, Mother, I'll see you in a while. I'm just going off for a while to be by myself — I'll be back before very long.'

Mother said, 'There she goes again! If you tell me it's true, she'll be home sadder and wiser.'

But old Angus never said a word. He just sat and smoked his pipe. And he still had this — as if a lump were in his heart. And he was under deep depression, just didn't want to get up, just wanted to sit. He had this great terrible feeling of loss.

So Mary rowed the boat over to the island. And he sat by the fire and he smoked and he smoked and he smoked. Maggie called him for dinner and the day passed by, but Mary never returned. Evening meal came, Mary never returned. Her mother began to get worried.

She came down and she said, 'Angus, has Mary come home? It'll soon be time for milking the cow again.'

'No,' he said, 'Mary has never come.'

'Perhaps,' she said, 'she — would you go down and see if the boat's in? Has she tied up the boat? Maybe she walked down to the village.'

Angus went out and there was no sign of the boat. 'No,' he said, 'the boat – '

'Well, she's not home. If the boat's not home, she's not home,' she said. 'I doubt something's happened to her . . . I doubt something's happened to her — Angus, you'll have to go and see what, you'll have to go out to the island. Go down and get Lachy's boat and go out to the island and see.'

So Angus goes down, just walks down and takes Lachy's boat, never asks permission, just pulls the rope, unties the rope and jumps in the boat. He doesn't — he had the feeling that he doesn't even worry what happens, he's so upset. And he rows out to the island and there's Mary's boat. And he pulls the boat in because the beach was quite shallow. And he lays the boat beside Mary's boat, his own boat. And he walks up the path, over the little hillock, down by the big rock to the little bay and the green patch beside the big rock, and walks right down where he saw the seal. He looks. The side of the rock was splattered with the blood where he had shot the seal. And he walks round the whole island, which wasn't very big, walks the whole island round — all he saw was a few spots of blood. Nowhere did he find Mary. Mary had completely disappeared, there wasn't a sign of her, not even a footprint. And he walked round once, he walked round twice and he went round a third time; every tree, every bush, every rock he searched, but Mary was gone.

And he felt so sad, 'What could happen to Mary, my poor wee Mary, what happened to her?'

Then at the very last he came back once again to the rock where he had shot the seal — and he looked out to sea, the tide was on the ebb. And he stood, looked for a long long while. And he looked at the rock, saw the blood was drying in the sun. And he looked again, then — all in a moment up come two seals, two grey seals, and they come right out of the water, barely more than twenty-five yards from where he stood! And they look at him. They look directly at him — then disappear back down in the water. And he had this queer feeling that he was never going to see Mary any more.

So he took his boat and he rowed home, tied up his boat. Just the one boat, took his own boat, left Lachy's boat on the island. He sat down beside the fire. His wife Margaret came to him.

She said, 'Did you see Mary?'

'No,' he said, 'I never saw Mary. I never saw Mary, I searched the entire island for Mary and Mary is gone. And look, between you and me, she's gone for ever. We'll never see Mary again.'

And they waited and they waited, and they waited for the entire days of their lives, but Mary never returned. And that is the end of my tale.

THE FISHERMAN AND HIS SONS

Having been reared on the West Coast, I had come in contact with many people who were descendants of the people whom the stories were about! This story I heard from an old country-man Duncan MacVicar when I was about fifteen and working in Achinagoul. Now Duncan lived in this farm cottage. It was primitive, no water, no toilet, kind of a bothy affair. But the farm was nearly a thousand acres. There used to be about five crofts in the place, but as the crofters went out Duncan bought the land and turned it into one great big hill farm. I made Duncan's bed, I cooked his meat, I was his butler, worker, chef, a man of all trades. Old Duncan MacVicar was a second daddy to me, but he was a big farmer. There was nothing that old Duncan did that I didn't know. And he told me one day about this large family.

THERE ONCE LIVED THIS CROFTER in Argyll and his was a large croft on the coast with a good wee bit of land. And the old man had done a bit of fishing when his children were small. Now he had five sons all together, and when they grew up there wasn't enough work on the croft to keep the five of them plus the father, who was getting a wee bit up in years and tired of fishing. So they sat down at the table one evening and discussed their future.

The young lads said, 'Well, Father, there's not much work for us here between the croft and the fishing.'

One lad said, 'We'll have to try and work out an agreement or we'll have to move out and find employment somewhere else.'

Now the old man didn't want his sons to go away and leave him because it was a large house. They had a good boat, and they had some cattle, some sheep and a couple of horses. So this one evening while the five lads and their mother sat at the table, he said, 'Well, sons, I've thought it over. Now I'm getting kind of up in years, the best thing I could do is turn the boat over to you three young ones and let you make a kirk or a mill of it!' (Meaning 'win or lose,' see!) 'Me and your two brothers, I think we could manage to run the croft between us. Whatever you make from the sea is your own — maybe help out your mother with a few pounds for your keep.' Because fishing in these days was really good.

So they made an agreement, the two oldest brothers would work on the croft with their father and the three youngest ones would take over the boat and the nets, work on the sea. The three young lads were to do nothing on the croft, the father and the two oldest sons were to do nothing on the shore.

Everything fared well. Now they stayed at the side of this sea loch and it could be pretty rough water sometimes. But across from where they stayed, maybe two miles out, there was an island. And this was a good wee lump of island. There was no habitation on it but it was a home for the seals, hundreds of them.

The old man, when his family was young, used to sail round the island, fish round it, set his nets. Sometimes when he came out and pulled up his nets, maybe a fish was halved through the middle, a big cod was eaten by a seal. He would just catch it, throw it back in the water. 'Ach well,' he would say to himself, 'the poor creatures need a bite like myself.' He never complained about one single thing to his old woman. Life went on like that till he finally gave up the boat to the three lads.

Now the three young men took over the fishing, set their nets, had a good fishing, sent their fish into the market. There was a village and a pier not far away where people sold their fish. Because along the whole West Coast in these days every little village had fishing boats, some had big boats, some only had sailing boats without engines. And they all had the posts up along the shore for drying nets. So the three young men did pretty well for the first two or three months. But then it started — the seals began to start on their fish — holes in their nets, good fish eaten in half, some with only tails and heads stuck in the net where the seals had eaten them. So every time they came back home at night-time to their father (they all stayed in the one big house, there were none of them married) and sat down to their supper, they would start to complain.

'Well, boys,' the father would say, 'how did you get on today, how did the fishing go?'

'Ach, not too good, Father,' his son said, 'not too good. The problem is those seals! If it wasn't for the seals we could make a good living.'

The father said, 'Boys, I've worked these shores long before you were born and after, when you were only children. And I managed to rear you up to young men to take care of yourselves. I got my share of the fish, and the share that I didn't get the seals got. They have families, you know, they have to feed their young too, as well as you! And the best thing you could do is leave these people alone.' The old man called them 'people'.

'Father,' the son said, 'it might be all right with you in your time, but now times are different. Times are changing. You are all right on the land, you and our brothers, our two older brothers are making a living. But we've to depend on the sea for our livelihood, and if it wasn't for these seals we could do better.'

Father said, 'Look, boys, I'm going to tell you once and tell you only once; I don't want you coming back here every night and complaining to me about the seals! Because the seals are my friends and always will be. Take what you can get and be thankful. Stop complaining about the seals or if you don't — I'm only telling you — it could be worse for yourselves.'

The young men never paid any attention to their father. 'Ach, he's getting old,' they talked among themselves. 'He doesn't understand, he's quite happy with the croft and our brothers.' But they carried on fishing. Some days they had were good, some days were bad, some days their nets weren't touched, some days their nets were cut where the seals went right through them. Some days the fish were destroyed, good fish in the nets. This began to get the young men down. They never complained to their father any more, but they complained among themselves.

They used to sail round the island, and they saw, about six or seven o'clock in the evening, that the seals would all come out on the rocks and hobble into this wee bay. Hundreds of them! On the face of the island were steep cliffs where the gulls used to nest. The boys had gathered eggs here when they were young. But a small bay went into the island, a cove where all the driftwood had piled up and the grass grew close to the rocks. You couldn't go any further into the island unless you climbed the rocks, a hundred and fifty feet up the cliff face. There was only one way into this bay, from the sea; there was no way you could come in from the land. It was sheltered and this is where the seals used to come, lie and bask in the evening.

So one evening the three young men came in early from the fishing. They made up a plan that they would take clubs, go and kill all the young seals they could find and stone the big seals to death. Try and rid the island of them. They never spoke a word to their father but just walked out, said they were going to check on their boat. The two older brothers, sitting by the fireside after working hard all day on their wee bit of land, never paid any attention. They were reading books, maybe the Bible, or reading the paper. The old mother was baking and the old father was lying back in his chair, maybe half asleep.

The three young men slipped away. Quietly they took their boat, rowed out to the island with their clubs. They went round the island first, then rowed into the small cove. When they landed there wasn't a seal to be seen, not one.

'Brother,' one said, 'it's queer, it's queer. There's always plenty of them.' After rowing about two miles to the island, they weren't going to row back straightaway, see!

They said, 'We'll wait.' And one said, 'They're bound to come in on the rocks some time this evening because they always do!' Even after the sun set, after they'd been eating all day, they came up to rest on the rocks. Young seals, half-grown seals, baby seals, old seals, all kinds climbed up on to the top of the rocks. Some swam into the bay and climbed up on this wee grassy cove. This is where the boys had pulled up their boat.

So they walked in on the grass, they cracked and talked for a wee while about what they were going to do. 'Well,' says one of the brothers, 'if we're going to wait, we'll have a small fire. We could sit here till the seals come up the rocks. Then we'll knock hell out of them with stones, stone them to death! And the ones that we can reach we'll kill with our clubs.'

So that they wouldn't be seen, they went further into this wee cove to a sheltered corner where all the driftwood had piled up. They kindled a small fire and sat down. They were talking and smoking, waiting for the seals. They waited maybe an hour.

The youngest said, 'Shst, listen! Listen! I hear something.'

'Oh,' one said, 'it's prob'ly the seals coming in.'

'No,' he said, 'it's no seals — it's voices!'

'Voices?' the other said. 'There's nobody here. Nobody here, there's no voices here. It can't be people because there's no people. Very seldom people.'

But they heard voices coming closer. Voices were coming closer — all in a moment they were surrounded by a colony of folk. There must have been a hundred and fifty, all came in behind them. Now there was no escape except up the cliff face.

The three young men sat with a wee fire and they looked. They didn't know what to do. They were aghast. They'd never seen people like this before — dressed in furry kind of suits. And talking among themselves, some talking in half Gaelic, half broken English and Gaelic. Now the boys themselves had good Gaelic and could understand some of what they were saying. There were voices said, 'That's them, they're the ones!'

The three young men stood up — didn't know what to do because there were too many of them. There were young ones, young boys, young lassies, bairns, wee toddlers, old women and old men! A hundred and fifty folk surrounded these young men. There's no escape, no way! This big one, the biggest of the lot, walked forward. The boys could see he was grey in the hair and dressed in these droll kind of furry clothes, the likes of which the boys had never seen in their lives before. They were terrified! They were only young men in their teens, you know! They didn't know what to do.

And this big one stepped forward. I'll say what he said but I can't say it the way he said it. 'Well, young men,' he said, in broken English and Gaelic mixed, 'you came here tonight on a purpose.'

They couldn't speak — were dumbfounded.

And he said, 'Your purpose was here — for to come and stone the seals to death — us, stone us! Kill our children and destroy our babies.'

And the oldest of the three brothers said, 'Sir . . . but you are not seals. We have never interfered with you . . . where do you come from? We've never seen you before. How can you condemn us for destroying the seals which has got nothing to do with you?'

And this man said, 'You have come here to stone the seals. We are the seal-folk and you have come here to destroy us! You meant, everything you intend to do is upon us. So we came here tonight to do the same thing to you.'

The seal-folk all gathered round each other. They mumbled and they talked, mumbled and talked among each other. Now these three young men are terrified! The older folk gathered round and had this meeting. Finally they said, 'We've held court and we're going to stone you to death, do the same thing, what you were going to do to us. You've been condemned to death, the same you promised us — there's no escape for you!'

The young men didn't know what to do. They tried to make excuses but it was no good. Then all in a minute, behind them came hobbling up, with a piece of driftwood under one arm, an old man with a long white beard, dressed in the same kind of furs, droll kind of skin.

'Stop, stop, stop!' he said in Gaelic. And the boys knew what he was saying.

The spokesman, the biggest man with the grey hair, said, 'What is it, Grandfather?'

'Stop!' he said. 'Wait!' The old man came up to the front, stood before the young men. 'Young men, you know what you've come here to do tonight. You came here to destroy us seal-folk, us people, and stone us to death. Well, probably you wouldn't have stoned us all to death, you could have hurt some of our children or destroyed some of our babies. But my son here wants me to wreak revenge upon you. Now,' he said, 'your father warned you many many times to leave us people alone! We take some fish from your nets because they're floating in the water, we take them from the net because there's many many more in other places to catch, apart from around here. What is round this island we say is ours.'

The three young men were too flabbergasted to speak, they couldn't talk back for themselves.

'But,' he said, 'I'm going to let you go this time with a warning. Remember what I tell you!' So he turns round to all the other folk and says to this oldest son of his, 'Listen, son, I want you to let these young men go.'

'But, Father,' he says, 'you know what they have come to do!'

'Son,' he said, 'remember one thing; if it wasn't for the young men's father, *you* or me wouldn't be here today — that's why I want to give them a chance. I never tellt you this before, but I'm going to tell you now.'

'Well,' the son said, 'you'd better make it good!'

'I'll tell you,' he said. 'Many many years ago when I was a young seal, I was tangled in that children's father's net and rope — I went in for a fish and I was. caught. He pulled me up and he set me free. Now,' he says, 'I want you to set these young men free. Now,' he says, 'remember, young men, we are the seal-folk. You leave us alone and we'll leave you alone!'

So they stepped back one and all. And the three young men ran to their boat and jumped in. They rowed as fast as they could. When they came back that night and beached their boat, walked into their father's house, they were as white as ghosts. The father looked, and they could hardly speak.

The father said, 'Well, sons, where have you been?'

'Oh, Father,' one said, 'we were out on the island, on Seal Island, there for a while looking around to see if . . . to find a good fishing spot.'

'And, boys, did you find a good spot that would suit you?'

'No, Father,' he said, 'I don't think so. We didn't find a good spot. It doesn't look very good. It looks kind of rough. In fact, I think in the future we'll take your word for it and keep away from Seal Island — leave the fish there,' he said, *'for your sea-folk.'* And that's the end of my story!

SILKIE'S FAREWELL

Now this happened to me a long time ago when I was only thirteen years old working with an old fisherman, Duncan Campbell. I think old Duncan had a notion to me because I was called Duncan. He was an elderly man in his late sixties, and he and I used to dig bait together for his fishing. We used to row his little boat from Furnace to Minard at the graveyard there. It was a big beach and if you landed too early you had to wait till the tide went out. As we sat there by the seaside we watched the popping heads of the seals which is a wonderful thing to see. I said, 'Duncan, my friend, there are many strange stories about the seal people.' And he told me this story.

IN A SMALL VILLAGE on the West Coast of Scotland there lived an old man called Angus MacLean and his wife Margaret. They had a small croft by the seaside, just a kind of rough little piece of croft. They had some arable land on which they grew a little potatoes and some vegetables, just to keep for themselves. But beside where they lived was a small island. And out on the island was the home of the seals. During the incoming tide this island would be surrounded with the sea. And there the seals would lie and bask in the sun. Now Margaret was the school teacher. She taught school in the local village. Everyone loved and respected Angus MacLean and Margaret his wife. They never had any children of their own. But they had one obsession — they loved the seals. And any spare time they had when the tide was low they would walk to the little island and walk among the seals. Now because they were so accustomed to walking among the seals, the seals of course paid them little attention. Now if you would walk to an island of seals and view them, the first thing when the seals see you appear they will disappear into the sea! And all you'll see is a little head floating around. You will love to see them staring out with their beautiful dark eyes. For Margaret and her husband this was the most fantastic time of their life.

After a while Margaret retired from teaching school. And Angus ran the small croft. He had a little hay which he used to cut, for he kept a couple of cows, and a few sheep and a few goats. But as I told you, their obsession was the seals. They knew every one by name. Out on the island they would say, 'There's old Angus, there's old Donald and there's old Hugh.' And of course the seals knew the visitors coming there, because no one else ever came to the small island apart from themselves. And the seals became accustomed to them. Then one sunny afternoon as the tide was full out Margaret and Angus walked down round the island.

Oh, there were baby seals sitting on the rocks sunning themselves. There were old seals, old cow seals lying around. And Margaret said, this is such-and-such, and Angus said, that's such-and-such. But then they came around a little corner of the island, and there lying on the top of a rock was an old seal. As they walked up they could see there was something wrong. His right flipper had been split all the way down. And he was lying — an open wound. Angus rushed over.

He says, 'Margaret, come and see this!' Margaret walked over. The old seal lay, his flipper split all the way down.

She said, 'He must have been hit with a boat or something, the propeller of a boat passing by. Angus, we can't leave him like this.'

'No, my dear,' he said, 'we are not going to leave him.' And Angus took off his jacket. He said, 'Margaret, look for two long pieces of driftwood.' And Margaret ran along the shore. She found two long pieces of wood. And he shoved them up the sleeves of the jacket. He made a little stretcher, and they lifted the old seal, put him on the jacket.

She says, 'Angus, what are we going to do with him?'

He says, 'Do with him? We're taking him home with us to the house. And I'm going to take care of him. We can't leave him lying here like this.' So between them they carried the old seal home to their little croft.

Angus says, 'Margaret, put him on my bed.' On his bed on top of the bed covers they placed the old seal. And Angus went in and got a needle and a piece of thread. He heated the needle over a little lamp, sterilised it. Very carefully he pulled the skin together and sewed it up, the whole flipper all the way up. And he took a little ointment he used for the cows' teats and things like that. He rubbed it in. He said, 'Margaret, I think he'll be all right.'

But she said, 'Angus, what are you going to do with him?'

'Do with him?' he says. 'I'm going to keep him here till he's well.' Of course Margaret was a loving old woman. They were devoted to each other. So to make a long story short they took care of the seal, nursed him and they fed him. Little tidbits at first because he wouldn't eat very much. But then he began to sit on the floor. And his flipper began to heal. A crust of a scab began to come. They fed him tidbits of fish and anything he could eat, saw that he was well took care of, gave him a drink of fresh water. They tended him like a child, a sick child. And a couple of weeks were to pass and his flipper healed. A large black scab came on it. And Angus checked it very carefully every day.

137

Till one morning he says, 'Margaret, I think it is time we'd better put him back to the sea. Now he's well enough to take care of himself.' So with the same stretcher from his jacket they carried him back again, placed him on the island. But then there came a terrible storm. Oh, it lashed for days and weeks. And Margaret and Angus couldn't get near the island in their spare time. The storm lasted for weeks, five weeks at least. The whole winter passed.

But then the spring began to come in. It was now about the month of May. And of course Angus had to cut a little hay for his goats and his sheep and his cow to keep the milk in the little croft where they lived. He and Margaret had spent a lonely winter together. They had never gone back to the island. And then for some strange reason Margaret took very sick. I don't know what the sickness was, but Angus was very upset.

She lay in her bed. And of course they called the doctor from the village. And the village being small, everyone knew Margaret because she had taught in the school. Everybody was upset. The doctor went down and he examined Margaret. He sat there beside Angus.

'Angus,' he said, 'this is strange. I don't know what's wrong with her.' But Margaret deteriorated as the days went past. And then she was in some kind of a coma. Till one day the doctor came for a visit and he pulled Angus aside. He said, 'Angus, I'm really sorry. There's not much more I can do.' Angus was very upset.

This was his childhood sweetheart, his wife he'd spent his life with! They had grown old together. He was so upset. They didn't have any family. Of course the villagers said this and said that. But no one could comfort Angus the same way. He sat there, lonely old man, for nights sitting by her bed holding her little hand as she lay in a coma. But one night there came a terrible storm. Thunder crashed. Lightning flashed. And then there was a quietness. But Angus was still sitting by his wife's bedside. Then — he heard a knock on the door — someone knocked. 'Who could this be at this time of night?' thought Angus.

He got up from the bedside because the small house he lived in was a croft and the door was very close to the bedroom of his wife. He walked to the door and he opened it up. There stood an old man with a long dark coat. Angus said, 'Hello there, could I help you?'

He said, 'Sir, yes, you really could help me. You see, I am an old man and I've been travelling all night long in this storm. And I'm looking for a little place to rest myself. Or a little work. Have you any little jobs you would have around?' This was the month of May, even though it was stormy season. And Angus taking care of his wife, his little hay was overgrown. It should have been cut. Angus knew this.

He said, 'Well, old fellow,' because the old man looked older than Angus. Angus could have been in his fifties. The old man looked in his sixties or seventies. Tall and old and bent with a long dark coat. He said, 'Old fellow, yes, I have work. But you see, there's not much way I could help you. Because you see, my wife is very ill. And I've been tending to her. I've got to sit by her bedside. I need someone to help me. Would you come in?' And he brought the old man into the house.

Angus looked at the man and saw that he was very old. He didn't have a beard but had this long grey hair and a long, dark coat reaching to the floor. And the funniest thing that Angus looked at was the eyes. They were the most brown and bright eyes he had ever seen! Like brown shining berries. And Angus had never looked into eyes like this before. Then he remembered — he had seen eyes like this before — but not in a human. He'd seen them in his friends the seals whom he missed. On the island he'd never paid attention to for a long time.

But anyway, the old man said, 'I'm only looking for a few jobs, if you've any you could have for me. I'll do anything for you. Just for my keep.'

And Angus said, 'You're just the person I need. The spare room — '

'Oh,' the old man said, 'no spare room for me. Do you have a barn?'

'A barn?' said Angus. 'What do you need a barn for?'

'Well,' the old man said, 'you see I want to be by myself. And I don't want to trouble you and your wife if she's not well. I'll work for you but I'll need to rest in your barn.'

'Oh,' Angus said, 'I've a barn but I couldn't have you sleeping there if you're going to work for me!' Angus was a very gentle kind of man, a loving kind of soul and he treated every one like himself.'

The old man said, 'What is your name?'

He said, 'Angus.'

'Well,' he said, 'Angus, look, all I require is a little sleep in the barn. Tell me what I have to do for you.'

Angus said, 'Well, the problem is my hay. You see, my wife being unwell I have never been able to cut it. And without my hay my animals will not survive this winter.'

'Och, I'm sorry,' says the old man, 'about your wife. But anyhow, if you show me where I could rest myself . . . you see, I've come a long way.'

Angus said, 'Would you like something to eat or drink?'

The old man said, 'No, Angus, I'm not needing anything to eat or drink. Just a little place to rest!' Angus got a lamp and he walked to the barn. Now the barn was full of straw, common straw.

He said to the old man, 'I'm really ashamed of myself.'

The old man says, 'Angus, forget it! All I need is a little rest.' But the old man went into the barn and he said goodnight. Angus closed the door and he walked back into the house. He sat down by her bed. She was lying there in pain and still, as if in her death bed. But he was tired and felt sleepy. He went to his bed. Angus didn't sleep with his wife because she was ill.

When he rose to make his breakfast in the morning, which was a very simple breakfast, a plate of porridge or something, all he heard was the rasp, 'scartch, scartch' of a scythe on a sharpening stone. You know how old people used to scythe the hay? And you know the noise of a stone as it rubs up and down the blade? It was going 'scartch, scartch, scartch'. Angus looked out the window. There was the old man, still with his long coat, and he was sharpening the scythe. But Angus said, 'He's had no breakfast!' And he went out and said, 'Would you like to come and have some breakfast with me?'

The old man said, 'No, Angus, I'm fine! Just leave me.' And he sharpened the scythe. Scartching the stone — it was a beautiful sound! A bit like the noise of a corncrake. And Angus said, 'It's so strange. I wonder who the old fellow is. I wonder where he came from.' But anyway, Angus went back to sit by his wife's bedside. She could not eat, she could not drink. Just lying in a coma there in the bed.

But it was mid-day when the old fellow came and knocked on the door. He had put the scythe by the window. And Angus looked out the window and saw that half of the hay was cut in beautiful long rows as if he had done it himself. Now Angus was a scytheman. It takes a good person who can cut hay with a scythe well. And Angus said to himself, 'Whoever this old man could be, he can surely use a scythe!' Angus was so pleased. But the old man came to the door.

He said, 'Angus, I just want to talk to you.'

Angus said, 'Yes, would you like something to drink?'

'Oh no,' he said, 'I don't need anything to drink.'

'Would you like something to eat?'

He said, 'No, Angus, I would not. I want nothing to eat. I was only wanting to say, could I see your wife?'

'My wife?' said Angus. 'Why should you want to see my wife?'

'Well,' he said, 'you told me that she's very ill. I just want to see her.'

Angus said, 'There's not much to see. She's lying in bed.'

'I won't disturb her,' said the old man. 'Could I see your wife?'

Angus said, 'I don't think there's any harm in that.' And he led the old man into Margaret's bedroom. There lay Margaret with her little pale hands on the bed, the bed sheet down over her neck. And the old fellow stood and he looked at her for a wee while. Very carefully he reached over with an old gnarled hand and he caught her hand in his. And he held it for a moment . . . And Angus stood and looked. Then a strange thing happened. For Margaret opened her eyes, and she looked up at the old man standing there holding her hand. Her eyes were as bright as the eyes of a bird. She smiled and fell into a deep sleep. Angus was amazed. Who was this man? He knew as that old man held her hand something strange had happened.

The old man said, 'Angus, I think your wife is going to be fine. Do you have a cup in your house?'

'A cup?' said Angus. 'What kind of a cup?'

'Oh, a mug or something,' said the old man.

'Are you thirsty?' said Angus.

'Not really thirsty,' he said. 'But do you have a cup?'

'Come to the kitchen,' said Angus. In the kitchens in these bygone days hung all these old enamel mugs. The old man reached up and he took from the little cleek an enamel mug. He said, 'This will do fine.' And he walked away. Closed the door behind him and he was gone.

Angus said, 'I wonder why he didn't take a drink from me. He's maybe going to the stream. Maybe he likes the stream water.' But Angus sat there by his wife's bedside when the old man came back once again.

He said, 'Angus, I have something for your wife.'

Angus said, 'Something for my wife? My wife doesn't need anything. She's in a coma.'

He said, 'Not any more she's not! Look!' And he had this enamel mug in his hand he'd took from the kitchen. He'd been gone for about fifteen or twenty minutes. And he returned. Very carefully . . . He said, 'Angus, don't you worry, your wife is going to be all right.' And he reached over and put his arm round her neck. He lifted her head up. He held this cup to her mouth. And to the amazement of Angus she drank from the cup. Even though her eyes were closed. After she drank from the cup for a few moments she opened her eyes, and smiled at the old man once again. She fell into a sleep. And the old man said, 'It's all right, Angus, don't worry. Nothing's going to happen!' And he took the cup. He walked back, and instead of putting it on the cleek he placed it on the kitchen table. He said, 'Now I'll have to go and finish my cutting of the hay.' He walked away and picked up the scythe. And he started 'scartch, scartch, scartch' again, the most beautiful sound in the world.

Angus says, 'What's going on here? What did he give my wife to drink?' And Angus walked over to the cup and he picked it up. He could see that in the bottom of it there were little drainings that Margaret had never drunk. He looked at it, put it to his mouth and tasted it. Now Angus' father had been a fisherman. Angus had been a fisherman all his life. Now sometimes the old fishermen when they ran out of tobacco, they chewed the dried seaweed. When Angus tasted the dregs from that cup, that was exactly what he tasted — seaweed. But he drained it in his mouth. And he felt the most tasteful sensation in the world! He placed the cup on the table. He says, 'What's going on here?' But that was only the beginning.

That night the old man never came to the house. He put the scythe by, went back to the barn, closed the door. The next day he came again for the same cup. For three days he carried that cup of liquid to Margaret's bedside and gave her a little drink. Angus didn't know what was going on. But he knew something strange was happening. On the third day he was sitting there. He looked up. The old man was finishing the last drop of hay that was cut in all these beautiful swathes, finishing the last rows.

Then a voice called, 'Angus, I'm hungry!' Angus rushed into the bedroom. And Margaret was sitting up in bed. She said, 'Angus, have you not got anything to eat? I'm starving!'

He said, 'Margaret, my love, you're starving? You're well?'

'Well?' she said. 'I'm hungry! Why didn't you call me for breakfast this morning?'

Angus said, 'Margaret!' And he threw his arms around her. The tears ran down his cheeks. He said, 'My love, love of my heart, you are well!'

She says, 'Well? I need something to eat. Bring me my clothes till I dress myself and make my own breakfast!'

He said, 'The love of my heart, you won't make your own breakfast! I'll get anything you want.'

'Oh,' she said, 'bring me some porridge or eggs or something. I'm starving!' Angus couldn't wait. He rushed into the kitchen. His fingers were fumbling. He fumbled with the stove, he fumbled with the fire. His wife was well! She was crying for food. He made her a little breakfast and brought it in and put it on her bedside. She sat there and filled herself up. She says, 'Angus, why didn't you bring me my breakfast earlier?'

He says, 'Margaret, you've been ill for three long weeks.'

'Well,' she said, 'I'm not ill! Get me my clothes!' After she finished her breakfast Margaret dressed herself. And got up. She said, 'I suppose there'll be a mess in the kitchen now!'

Angus said, 'No, my dear, there's no mess in the kitchen.'

And she said, 'Why aren't you cutting the hay?' And she

looked out the window. She saw the hay all lying cut. She said, 'Angus, who's been cutting the hay?'

He said, 'An old friend of mine.'

'Well,' she says, 'bring him in. And give him a cup of tea!'

'I'll just do that, Margaret,' he said. And he went to the door and called the old fellow before him. He came up, took the scythe and stuck it in the corner of the barn. The old fellow took the sharpening stone that he'd been using and stuck it in beside the scythe. And he came in.

He said, 'Well, Angus, now I think that's time I should be on my way.'

'Angus, who's this old man?' said Margaret.

'Oh, my dear,' he said, 'you know that you've been unwell.'

'I've never been unwell,' says Margaret. 'I've been asleep!'

'Well,' he said, 'he's been helping me cut the hay.'

She said, 'Give him something to eat or something to drink!'

And the old man said, 'No, my dear, I'm not needing anything to eat or anything to drink.'

'Well, Angus,' she said, 'give him some money! Pay the old man if he wants to be on his way.'

Angus said to the old fellow, 'I must thank you very much. You made a wonderful job of my hay.'

'Well,' the old man said, 'I've just come to help you when you were in trouble.'

'And now,' Angus said, 'I'll go and get your pay.'

And the old man said, 'Pay? What do you mean, pay?'

Angus said, 'Well, you cut my hay! And you've stayed with me while my wife was sick.'

But Margaret said, 'I was not sick — I don't remember anything.'

The old man said, 'I don't need any pay for anything. You've already paid me, you know.'

'Paid you?' said Angus. 'You've never had a bite here in this house, and you've been here for three days! And now you refuse to accept pay from me? I will pay you right now!' said Angus.

The old man said, 'No, Angus, you won't pay me, and never a penny!' He pulled up his sleeve. There from the top of his arm right to the back of his hand was a great big scar. He said, 'Angus, there's my pay.' And the old man walked away.

SILKIE'S FAREWELL

Angus threw his arms around Margaret. He said, 'Margaret, my darling, I think it's time I should tell you a story.' And Angus told the same story to Margaret I'm telling you.

Editor's note

OF THE HUNDREDS OF TRADITIONAL STORIES Duncan Williamson tells to audiences of enthralled listeners every week of the year in classrooms, halls and by firesides across the country — the tales highest in demand, by far, are those of the seal people. In an increasingly materialistic, mechanised and complex world, these stories of seals, the seal-folk, preserve simply and dramatically lessons for survival. Duncan Williamson was himself born in a tent on the shores of Loch Fyne in Argyll in 1928, and he has spent his entire life as one of Scotland's Travelling People, formerly called tinkers. The 'travellers' of today are a minority group of several thousand families who live naturally, close to the land and sea, following seasonal work and not bound to dwelling in any one place. Their stories are as close to the world of the supernatural as any can be, because this Other World is the one travelling people believe some day they will join.

Duncan left home in Argyllshire at the age of fifteen and travelled on foot into the mainland, then north into Fraserburgh. He took with him silkie stories he had learned from Gaelic speaking crofters and fishermen of the West Coast. And he would ask Scots speaking sailors and fishermen of the East Coast, did they have any seal stories? Many were indeed known in Morayshire and Buchan in the 1940s and 1950s.

The first collection of stories about creatures of the Other World by Duncan Williamson was *The Broonie, Silkies and Fairies* (Canongate, 1985 and Harmony Books, New York, 1987). The present collection contains five silkie, or seal-folk, stories from this first book. Four of these I have not anglicized, because their dialogues in Scots represent the linguistic diversity of the tradition. The present collection compares with the earlier in that all the stories have a moral purpose, a religious core. They are a matter of teaching to show what happens to you if you are evil and bad, or, good and kind. The finest stories, however, do not have right and wrong clearly spelled out. There is always a sense of mystery, the 'message' leaving a lot to your own intelligence. 'Happy ever after' endings are very rare.

147

Seven recently recorded stories of silkies have been written down verbatim from Duncan's narrations to make up the core of *Tales of the Seal People*. 'The Silkie Painter' was originally published under the title 'The Old Woman and the Silkie' by Collins as winner of the Scottish Short Story award in 1984. It was subsequently reprinted in *The Fiction Magazine* (Feb 1985) and in the *Beloit Fiction Journal* (Fall 1989). 'Mary and the Seal' was first published in *Fireside Tales of the Traveller Children* (Canongate, 1983 and Harmony Books, New York, 1985). All fourteen stories may be listened to with permission from the archivist or the director of the School of Scottish Studies, Edinburgh University; the original taped recordings are lodged in the School's Sound Archives.

Linda Williamson
Peat Inn, Fife
January 1992

Glossary

bachle	troublesome person
bare than busy	all one can manage
ben	further in
bing	take (cant)
cam	came
canny	careful
ceilidhs	song and story get-togethers (Gaelic)
clinker-built	made of interlocked strips of wood, typically Norwegian
country hantle	non-travellers (cant)
cowp	overturn
cracked	discussed news
cratur	creature, dear one
doubt	fear, expect
dram	drink of whisky
forbyes	as well (as)
gadgie	man (cant)
graip	iron-pronged farming fork
greetin and roarin	crying and shouting
gurie's	girl's (cant)
hantle's	folk's (cant)
kinchen	child (cant)
knowe	hillock
oxter	under the arm; lend an arm to someone in walking
ron	seal (Gaelic)
saltie	a sailor, fond of the sea
sappy soukers	shoots of the young ash plant
scartch	make a scraping, rasping noise
shanness	Shame on you! (cant)
silkie	seal-person (cf. selch, seal)
sprachled	clamboured
two-three	a few
wir	our